LOST IN Secrets

Wenna Olsson

To any who has ever felt lost in the emotions that consume like waves. You're seen. You're not alone.

Prologue 7

Chapter 1 13

Chapter 2 22

Chapter 3 29

Chapter 4 37

Chapter 5 44

Chapter 6 54

Chapter 7 62

Chapter 8 65

Chapter 9 74

Chapter 10 84

Chapter 11 91

Chapter 12 100

Chapter 13 109

Chapter 14 117

Chapter 15 127

Chapter 16 133

Chapter 17 142

Chapter 18 152

Chapter 19   162

Chapter 20   170

Chapter 21   178

Chapter 22   188

Chapter 23   198

Chapter 24   207

Chapter 25   214

Chapter 26   221

Chapter 27   229

Chapter 28   235

Epilogue   244

Thank you!   248

About the Author   249

Acknowledgments   250

Prologue

Age 10

Little teal-painted toes peeked back at me as I watched my sandals push off the wood floor, swaying the porch swing back and forth. Sweet smells of an arriving summer lingered in the air, and a thrill of excitement flittered in my belly.

It was the last week before summer break.

The screen door closed, and Mom walked over to sit next to me while I waited for the bus. Her long chestnut hair hung in a braid over her shoulder, and the sparkle in her cerulean eyes matched the smile across her lips. She sat down, her hand patting my knee with a little squeeze.

"Are you excited about our upcoming trip?" she asked.

She meant our annual year-end celebration—a family trip to the beach. We all looked forward to it, but mostly, Mom loved the beach.

"Of course! I'm so excited school is almost over. I'll get more time with you. And Daddy, too." I smiled back at her.

"I agree. It's what I look forward to most." Her finger lightly bopped my nose. "You have no idea how you've changed my life for the better, sweet girl," she said, leaning in to kiss my temple.

Before I had time to think about her words, my best friend, Beck, and two of his younger brothers—Ben and Conrad—came jogging up the steps to our porch.

"Hey, Mrs. Weber. Lissa." He nodded.

"Beckett, always such a pleasure to see you. And your brothers. How's your mother?" my mom asked.

Beck shoved his hands in his pockets. "Mom's good. Due to having Jasper any day now. So, she's not nearly as stressed as she normally gets around this time of year. No big travel plans this summer."

I perked up at Beck's response. The Cirillo family traveled internationally every summer, sometimes to more than one country. I loved Beck's stories of faraway places; they were always full of wonder, but it also made me sad that he wasn't here. They would be gone for over two months, leaving very little time for us to hang out during our summer break. So the fact he wasn't going anywhere this year was making me very happy. I was about to tell him when we heard the bus pull up at the end of the street.

"Bus is here," Conrad's little voice said, and he jumped the stairs before running down the sidewalk, Ben not far behind him.

"I'll see you later," Mom said, giving me a side hug as we stood. I grabbed my backpack off the floor and walked with Beck down the steps.

"Love you, Mom," I yelled, waving over my shoulder.

"Love you more, Alessia! Don't forget your father will pick you up from school today."

Beck and I continued our way to the bus.

"What do you mean you're not going away this summer," I asked him. The end of the street neared, bringing us to the door of the school bus.

Beck grinned at me. "I mean, my mom told me this morning we are staying here this summer. With the new baby, she didn't want the hassle traveling can sometimes give us."

I clapped my hands together, sprinted up inside the bus, grabbed the first seat I saw, and yanked Beck next to me. "Oh, this is such good news!" I beamed at him.

Beck chuckled, nodding his head. "Yep."

"This means we will be together the whole summer." I started chattering about everything I wanted to do now that Beck would be around to do them with me. "As soon as I get back in a couple of weeks after my family's trip, we can make a list and do all the things. Oh, this is going to be so great!"

Eager anticipation built inside of me. I loved spending time with Beck. We'd known each other ever since we were running around in diapers. He and I just made sense. We were always together, always looking for an adventure, always finding trouble. He was always there.

Beck laughed. "I know! It's going to be the best summer yet."

Releasing another frustrated breath, I sat on the bench outside my school and checked the time again. *Where is he? He was supposed to be here over an hour ago.*

Anytime Dad picked me up after school, he was never late. Dad liked to keep things in order; he was neat and efficient. He wasn't known for being late.

I pulled my phone out of my bag to try Mom and Dad for the third time. Neither of them answered. Annoyance turned to worry. *Did Dad forget? How could he forget? Something may have happened.*

The thought of calling the Cirillos crossed my mind, but at the same moment, Mrs. Cirillo's car pulled up to the curb near my bench. Her lips formed a frown, and her eyes glimmered with unshed tears. Something was very wrong.

Getting out of the car, she slowly approached me. One hand absently rubbed the large, round form of her belly, the other tucked stray black hairs behind her ear. "Alessia, we were asked to pick you up. We need to take you to the hospital," she said tenderly but also a note of concern.

Beck jumped out of the back of the still-running car and raced towards me.

"Lissa." Sadness broke his voice.

He sat beside me and grabbed my hands, folding them into his. "Come on, we have to go."

My concerned feelings grew.

A whimper came from Mrs. Cirillo before she covered her mouth with her hand. We followed behind her to the car and Beck opened the door for me.

The questions of what was going on flitted through my mind, but the only words that came were, "Where are my parents?"

Mrs. Cirillo glanced at me through the rearview mirror. "Your father asked that we come to pick you up," she said, clearing her throat. "There's been an accident." A slight tremble to her words.

"An accident?" What kind of accident? Mom? Or was it Dad? Is he okay?

"What are you saying?" I whispered. But if Dad told her to come get me, then he can't be that hurt, right? *Maybe it's not Dad.*

My heart stuttered and beat faster, my body restless. Beck grabbed one of my fidgeting hands, and my eyes drifted to look up at him.

We pulled into the parking lot of the local hospital. The Emergency sign loomed above its doors and the car turned off. Putting me in an uneasy silence. I took several deep breaths, unable to open the car door.

"Why are we here?" I asked no one in particular; I just needed my mind to stop racing. *Why would we be here? She said there was an accident, but how bad was the accident? It must be bad if we are here, right?*

"Better together?" Beck asked in response.

I watched his fingers squeeze a little tighter over mine.

"Better together," I said quietly, squeezing back.

Finally opening the door, we got out of the car and headed toward the entrance. Inside, Dad paced in the waiting room. Seeing Dad sent my nerves skyrocketing. *Where was Mom?*

I ran over to him. "Where's Mom? What happened? Mrs. Cirillo said there was an accident. Why didn't you call? Why are we at the ER?" My hands were shaking, so I tucked under my arms, wrapping myself in a hug. Dark and terrible thoughts surfaced answering all my questions.

Dad placed his hands on my shoulders, trying to calm me. "Alessia." His face winced, and he swallowed, trying to speak again. "Lessy, your mother...." He choked up, tears streaming down his face.

No. No, no, no, no. My eyes started burning, and my vision blurred. A trickle of wetness reaching my cheek. "Dad, what are you saying? Where's Mom? Why is she here?" My words came out a shaky mess.

Heavier tears came.

Where was my mom? Was she okay?

Dad sat on one of the seats, taking me with him. He was so sad. My heart hurt and I didn't know why.

"There was a car—ran a red light—your mother—your mother didn't survive the crash." Dad barely got the words out before he broke down into sobs. He fell back into the chair, covering his face with his hands.

I sat, watching my dad. It was as if I heard him but didn't believe him. Beck moved to stand next to the seat I was half sitting in. I turned toward him and looked at my best friend's grieving face. It was like he mirrored my own pain. He reached for a hug, and I stood to accept it.

Chapter 1

Seven years later

A light breeze lifted my long golden brown hair as I sat outside Beans n' Cream, waiting for my friend Ava to finish her excursion in the shoe store across the street. I loved fashion, but we had been at this all day, and it was well past lunch. *A girl needs to eat too.*

Taking a sip of my iced latte, I finally saw her cross the street. She plopped down in the seat across from me, looking classic Ava in her floral summer dress and strappy sandals.

"Ooh, that looks yummy! Where's mine?" Ava grinned, setting her generous amount of shopping bags down.

"I didn't know how long you would be." I shrugged. "But no worries. You can just order through the app, and they'll bring it right out," I told her, taking another bite of my turkey panini.

Ava ordered her drink and then began to tell me, in great detail, about all the amazing shoes she found after I bailed on her. I listened intently and admired her enthusiasm as she indulged in her retailing.

Ava was a fashion icon. Someone looked up. Others wanted to be like her. She had this way of making everyone she encountered feel special.

My first year at Ridgecrest Academy she pulled me into the seat next to her in my first class and told me I was always welcome to sit with her. She helped me feel accepted and not quite alone. That thoughtfulness meant a lot, and I quickly learned Ava was easy to talk to—somehow always understanding my grief—and from there, our friendship blossomed.

A Beans n' Cream staff member walked out and served Ava her drink. She thanked him. Then, turning inquisitive emerald eyes on me, she flipped some blonde hair behind her shoulder.

"So Tristan Dufort," she said, dripping with suspicion.

"What about him?"

"You said he's been practicing tennis with you." Her lips lifted in the corners, manicured nails playing with the straw of her cup.

"It's nothing. We've run into each other a few times on the tennis courts over the summer. He's just being nice and friendly." I shrugged my shoulders. "Helping me learn a few new tricks."

Ava chuckled. "See, that's what I'm talking about. I don't think I've ever seen you so ruffled by some guy."

"I'm not ruffled."

She threw me a doubtful look, and I picked up my phone, attempting to escape the conversation. How did I tell Ava his interest made me nervous. I didn't let others close easily.

"It's understandable, really. Tristan is like a god at Ridgecrest. One does not just talk to Tristan. Receiving his attention would make any girl weak in the knees," she said dreamily.

I considered her words. Was I taken by Tristan's charm? No, that wasn't it.

Ever since losing Mom, I lost a little of myself, too. So when Dad and I moved to Maple Grove three years ago, it was easier to not get too attached. *People couldn't hurt you if you didn't let them in.*

Her assumption on the few encounters I've had with Tristan wasn't a surprise, but it did make me wonder. *What if it was more for him? What if he liked me? No. No, that would be absurd. I am so not his type.*

"Ava, really?" I raised one brow.

"He's not the type to do things flippantly," she countered.

I sighed. "But why me? And even if he is interested in more, what makes you think I am?"

A deep chuckle crossed her lips, and her elbows leaned against the table, getting closer to me. "Why not. He's tall, great hair, lovely deep voice, and let's not forget he's a Dufort. And you. You're beautiful and an amazing person. Who's to say it just took him a little while to finally get some sense in his head."

"I don't know. Maybe. But we have more pressing matters than who Tristan Dufort is crushing on."

She gave me a questioning look and asked, "Like?"

I motioned to the large amount of shopping bags at our feet. "Like how we are getting all of this in your car."

We started laughing, gathered the copious amounts of bags, and headed toward the car.

Ava dropped me off at my house at the end of the street leading to the school grounds. A two-story grey brick style home. Far grander and larger than anything Dad and I needed, but that was the luxury of Ridgecrest Academy—the creme de la creme of college-prep boarding schools. They paid for everything when they offered Dad his job at the Academy.

In fact, Ridgecrest was the whole reason we moved my freshman year.

Four years after Mom died, just when I started to feel like I reached a good spot to deal with life, Dad received a teaching position at the prestigious prep school. Turning my life upside down. Again.

We moved to a different world on the other side of the country—the state of Washington all the way to tiny little Connecticut. It was a smart move for my dad. He grew exponentially in his career. It still astonished me how they found my dad and presented him with such an impressive position.

I, however, didn't see any of it as good.

After Mom died, life didn't just go back to normal. Normal no longer existed. I had a gaping hole in my life that would never be repaired. An impossible ache of wanting her to still be.

The drastic shift in Dad's behavior didn't help either. He wasn't the same. All his focus went into work, and our conversations became vague and shallow. It wasn't entirely his fault. I drew inward and hid. Hid from everyone but Beck. But the move took him away, too.

Entering the front door, I walked through the entryway to the kitchen, setting my bags on the island.

"Dad? I'm home."

I wondered if he was even home. He often would forget or never tell me his schedule. It made it hard to rebuild trust.

When we first moved, I was furious with him. Caring very little to have a relationship. But the sting of not having Mom nagged at my conscious too much, which helped me realize I only had one parent left and should appreciate what moments were still available. Over time, I slowly softened to the idea this was our new home and put efforts toward a new rhythm of life together, attempting to build bridges where possible. He received my attempts well enough and still struggled with putting work first, but I could tell he was trying.

"Dad, you here?"

I grabbed a glass and filled it with water from the faucet. When I turned around, I saw Dad strolling out of his office across from the kitchen.

He wore a white dress shirt and brown slacks, accentuating his lean length, and his dark brown hair was styled neatly. He walked toward me, his right hand fiddled with his glasses, appearing deep in thought.

"Hey, there you are." I smiled and offered him a glass of water, too. He nodded and sat on one of the bar stools.

"Alessia?" He paused, pondering. "What would you say to a weekend trip to the beach?"

I had a momentary lapse of disbelief. I wasn't sure I heard him right. The last time we went to the beach was eight years ago. *Not since Mom.*

"Um—I mean. A beach trip? Are you sure?" I fidgeted, my feet shifting, and tucked some of my hair behind my ear. I wondered if I should broach the subject of Mom. Instead, I said, "What's the occasion?"

My old therapist would say this was progress. Dad and I were taking steps to remember her and still building life moments together. At least, I think that's what she would say. But maybe that wasn't Dad's intent; he hardly talked about her anymore.

Dad tapped his fingers excitedly on the counter. "I've got some exciting news. Pack some things. We won't go far, just a few hours away. We'll leave tomorrow." He rose from his seat, humming to himself.

Well, that was odd.

Early afternoon the next day, we arrived at a cozy rental off the shore. No clue how he found something so nice still available this time of year, but I wasn't complaining.

While Dad went out to grab a few food items for the weekend, I put on my bikini and overlayed it with a light sundress. Pulling my hair into a messy bun, I made my way down to the sand with a blanket and a book.

Salty air filled my lungs, and crashing waves soothed and relaxed. There were quite a few people scattered around, but I found a spot not far out and spread my blanket across the soft sand.

A pinch of despair squeezed in my chest when I sat and gazed out at the endless path of water. *This probably was a bad idea.*

Everything about this trip had me too focused on the past. Too focused on the trip that never came to fruition. Because Mom wasn't there to make it happen.

They say the grief of losing a loved one gets easier with time, but it's not true. In reality, it never truly leaves us. Instead, the pain ebbs and flows like the ocean. Sometimes crashing waves and sometimes calm. It's been a painful life lesson learning how to keep my head above water during the storms.

My thoughts traveled down memory lane as I soaked in the sun's warmth. And that, unfortunately, brought to mind my fondness for another person, along with the sting of losing him.

Beckett Cirillo.

Beck was there. Through all of it. He crawled into my dark pit of sorrow with me and assured me he would sit there next to me until we could climb out together.

And he did.

He was a big part of why I didn't completely fall apart after Mom's death. It grew us even closer over the years, and as we got a little older I thought we might be something more, but then he slowly became distant, and then I moved.

I never heard from him after we left. I wrote him several letters over the years. Because that was something we would often do in school together: pass notes. But he never responded. Finally, after so long, I was tired of the disappointment of putting hope in something that was going nowhere, and I stopped writing. Even through the disappointment, though, Beck was part of my past, a treasured part. And I didn't know how to escape that.

Opening my eyes, I observed the area around me. It felt like someone was watching me.

Children played in the white sugar-like sand, umbrellas flapped in the wind, and several people walked along the edge of the waves. No one was taking any significant notice of me, though.

I shook my shoulders, seeking to chase away the creepy chills of being watched. But just as I started to turn my attention to my book, I saw him—a guy walking away from the shoreline a bit further down.

I squinted. The sun made it hard to make out any more than his profile. There was something, though. Something about him reminded me of....*it couldn't be him.*

Whoever it was disappeared from my sight, and I let out a heavy sigh. I decided my mind was playing tricks on me—considering I was just thinking about Beck—and I attempted to forget the whole thing by opening my book. *It couldn't possibly be him. And if it was, why would he be in Connecticut? Why would he be at this beach?*

That evening, we had dinner at a relaxed seafood bistro on the town's main street.

"So, this exciting news you wanted to talk about?"

"Yes. The Academy Director has informed me of an upcoming trip planned for September for my department. And they want to send me!" His excitement was tangible. He was practically on the edge of his seat.

I reached across the table and squeezed his hand. "That's so great! Where are they sending you? How long you think you'll be gone?"

"Director Langley said they have plans to cover my class schedule for the entire month. A team in Japan is developing some new technology. And Alessia, they want to include me in the developing process. In addition, they want me to build a new course around the project for Ridgecrest."

The more information he revealed, the more amazed I became. "Wow! Japan. New technology. Sounds so incredible, Dad! I'm really happy for you." I squeezed his hand one more time and returned to my meal. Then, a thought occurred to me. "Does this mean I'm going, too?"

Dad swallowed his bite of food and smiled. "Thank you! Ah, no, I don't believe so. I don't recall the Director mentioning the inclusion of family. I didn't think of it then, but you can manage a few weeks without me. I feel like you're the one caring for me most of the time anyway." He chuckled.

That was true; I did manage most of the household without him. But still, Japan was on the other side of the world, and I wasn't sure how I felt about being away from him that long at that distance. I wasn't going to let my worries spoil our celebration, though. So I smiled and continued eating. *These were good signs for your dad's career, Alessia. And it was only one month. So then, why do I still have this reluctant feeling about it?*

With full stomachs, we explored some of the shops on the main street. The street was packed with people. Signs at the end of the street kept it closed to traffic so people could enjoy an evening stroll. Stringed lights were displayed along the street, going back and forth between the buildings, highlighting the outside dining areas. Muffled conversations and children's laughter set the soundtrack as we walked, and Dad pointed out certain items he found unique.

One of those bells at the top of doors set to ring when someone opens it rang, catching my attention and causing me to look up.

Two shops down a young man was leaving a coffee shop, and my gaze lingered on him. Something in the way he moved drew my curiosity. I'm not sure why. I could only see his back, but the familiarity reminded me once again of Beckett Cirillo.

Chapter 2

Hazel eyes stared back at me as I applied my mascara and liner. I added some neutral tinted lip balm, fixed my hair in a ponytail, and grabbed my tote before walking out the door.

The first day of school arrived quicker than I was ready for. Dad's spontaneous trip away last week had me feeling off-kilter. Like thinking too much about the past was messing with my focus.

Wanting to take advantage of the last days of summer, I decided to walk the 10 minutes to the Academy. The 285-acre campus was located on the outskirts of town. It resembled more of an Ivy League university than a high school.

Ridgecrest was known for its wealth of academic departments with leading mathematics, science, engineering, and technology staff. It was also home to a dance and art studio and a world-class performing arts theatre. Not to mention the resources to accommodate every sport: a full-size football stadium, an 18-hole golf course, two Olympic-size pools, multiple tennis courts and soccer fields, a hockey rink, and a top-of-the-line gym facility and equipment.

This was where the rich and powerful sent their successors to prepare for life.

Where the prominent became even more prominent.

The acceptance rate was extremely low, putting the school enrollment around 435 students. It was only for the amazing deal they offered my dad that I managed to have a chance to be considered.

As I approached the final block leading to the academic wing entrance, the lush landscaping came into focus.

Massive oak doors hung open while the parking lot filled with non-resident students.

A shiny gold, extremely expensive car slowed and parked in the parking space nearest to the main doors. Tristan Dufort flawlessly exited his car, and his sharp green eyes instantly found me. Sandy brown hair in an intentional tousled look. Tall lean frame along with his confident stride portrayed the rich boy that he was.

Ava's "weak in the knees" comment came back to me, and it made sense. The boy was far too appealing to the eyes than anyone should be, even in his school uniform of a white dress shirt, checkered tie, and black tailored pants.

"Well, if it isn't my new favorite person," he said, coming around the car. His friend Andrew climbed out of the passenger seat behind him.

"Hey." I looked behind me. "Are you talking to me?"

He lifted his uniform jacket over his shoulder and gave me a breathtaking smile. "Who else would I be referring to? I was hoping I'd see your beautiful face this morning. Just wouldn't be right if I didn't."

Umm, is he flirting with me?

"Ha, yeah, maybe." I chuckled. Not that his attention wasn't flattering. It just seemed odd. We never spoke much before this summer. I would see him in the hallways, and we had a few classes together over the years, but we never talked. I didn't even know someone like him knew who I was.

"Really, Tristan. Why are you wasting your time with this?" Andrew said and pushed past us.

Tristan's lips turned down, his eyes watching his friend go into the school.

"He seems like a happy guy," I tittered.

His focus came back to me. Another smile.

"Just ignore him. I was thin—"

"Alessia, what are we doing out here?" Ava bounced down the steps from the school entrance. Voice all innocence. But she wasn't fooling anyone.

"Welp," I said while looping my arm into Ava's. "I'm sure I'll be seeing you later." I turned her around and walked inside.

"I knew it!" Ava whisper shouted as we worked our way around students into the building. I rolled my eyes and tugged her closer to my side to climb the first floor stairs, passing more students.

"Stop. He's just being a guy. Why would he suddenly have an interest in me? And if he is...trust me, it's not worth thinking too much on."

Ava looked like she didn't believe me. "I'll let it go. For now. Anyway, I have other tea to spill. Ridgecrest has two new students this year!" she sang, bobbing around a little with excitement.

We reached the top of the stairs, which divided into a T. Ava had her class to the right, and mine was to the left.

"Riveting, Ava," I muttered. "The late bell will be ringing any moment. Tell me later? Oh, and text me your schedule. I forgot it already." I turned the opposite way, waving to her. She cheerfully agreed and headed to her own first-period class.

Most of the seats were filled when I got to class. I grabbed a spot in the back row, preparing my things for the start of class.

A quick vibration came from inside my bag. Pulling my phone out, I checked Ava's text.

Ava: Here's the link - <u>Class Schedule</u>. Also, I haven't seen him yet, but word is that one of the new students is sooo finee.

My head shook at Ava's antics. About to send my reply, a hush settled over the room. I looked up, and as my eyes reached the front, my world stopped.

Speaking with the professor was a tall, dark-haired male. Who. I. Recognized. It was Beckett—my Beck.

Wait, that can't be right. Why would Beck be standing in my history class? Not only that, he was a year ahead of me. Shouldn't he have graduated last year? But it was definitely him. *What is going on?*

My spine straightened, and I cleared my throat. Looking around the room, the rest of the class seemed just as curious to Beck's presence as I was.

Finally, Professor Gibbon, a plump man with salt and pepper hair, nodded at Beck and addressed the class.

"Good morning, everyone! I see you have taken notice of our new student. Be sure to make him feel welcome. We're not accustomed to receiving new seniors. With that out of the way, welcome to your first day of school. I look forward to what our year together holds."

Beck turned toward the class, and our eyes met for the briefest moment. The joyful light I always associated with him wasn't there. He didn't even acknowledge me or sit near me. Instead, he chose a seat on the opposite side of the room.

Professor Gibbon's lecture continued in the background, my thoughts distracted with trying to figure out why on earth Beck was sitting 30 feet away from me. I wanted to talk to him, but apprehension from his response froze me. He clearly saw me and didn't choose the very open seat next to me. *Maybe he preferred the front? No, none of that matters. Why is he here?*

History ended, and Beck was up and moving so fast that he was gone before I could work up any courage to approach him.

My next three periods weren't any better.

I didn't see Beck again, but he never left my mind. Focusing on anything my professors had to say was a complete fail.

By lunch, I literally felt like I was going insane. My stomach was in knots. *Why is his being here having such an effect on me?*

The dining hall buzzed with the chatter of students gathering and sitting down to eat. I spotted Ava at one of the round wooden tables along the wall of scenic windows. I chose a plate of lo mein from the extensive food options before sitting down next to her.

"Can you believe this place? You'd think someone leaked a new school scandal. Like we never get new students? Well, I mean, I guess not in their senior year. But still, the shock and awe are so overdramatic, even for Ridgecrest," Ava said.

I gave her a confused look and asked, "What are you talking about?"

Ava straightened. "You can't be serious. The whole school has been acting brainless all day. Remember I told you about those two new students?"

I nodded.

"It's all anyone is talking about. How do you not know this?" She continued.

My brain must have been in more of a fog than I realized. I couldn't recall what my last three professors lectured on, let alone what students were gossiping about. I shrugged and said, "I hadn't noticed."

Ava opened her mouth to say more, but something caught her eye behind me. I turned my head to see what she was staring at.

At the entrance of the dining hall stood a gorgeous young woman. Her uniform fit her curves perfectly, her makeup flawless, and her kinky ebony hair rested around her shoulders. I'd never seen her before, that meant she must have been one of the new students.

She walked, turning heads at every table. None of the attention seemed to faze her—as was the case for most Ridgecrest students. A walk that said she owned this place and everything in it.

"Who is she?" I asked Ava, who was still staring in the girl's direction.

"I heard her name is Chelsea. Her family apparently just returned here from overseas. Some ambassador's daughter. They're here short term before they head back to France."

A moment later, Esme and Tate joined our table.

"You better have a good reason for ditching me last weekend," Esme said, pointing her fork at Ava.

Esme and Ava were cousins, and Tate was Esme's boyfriend. I usually only spent time with them when Ava did.

"Don't. It was a whole thing with my mother. I don't want to talk about it."

Ava switched up the conversation and started asking everyone how their day was, which returned me to my obsessive musings of Beck.

It was as if my mind conjured him into existence because, in my peripheral, I noticed Beck taking a seat a few tables away from ours. He didn't draw the same attention as Chelsea's entry, but there was still chatter around him.

Without effort, he initiated conversation at his table like he belonged. *How is he at Ridgecrest? And why didn't he stick around to say hi after history? This is stupid; just go say hi to him.*

I looked over at his table. *Okay, basically staring.*

Waiting for him to make eye contact and recognize I was there. His friend. The girl he said he would never forget.

Finally, after what felt like forever, I got my wish. Beck's eyes focused on me, and I was unprepared for the tingling sensation his attention stirred within me. *Were his eyes always so mesmerizing?*

They pulled me in and said they never wanted to let me go.

He nodded and broke the contact, returning to his conversation. No smile or wave; he just nodded.

I returned to finishing my food and attempted to focus on the conversation happening at my table. Far grumpier than I was a second ago.

Beck and I haven't spoken since I moved here. And he never responded to any of the letters I sent him, but I couldn't help the feeling of regret that crept in. I had so many questions. But my biggest one was: Were Beck and I no longer friends?

Chapter 3

The first week back was a slow agony of torture. Turned out Beck was only in my history class; I didn't see him much outside of that class and lunch. And it was like he was intentionally trying to avoid me.

The constant feeling of not knowing, not understanding was getting to me. I couldn't figure him out. I wanted so badly to talk to him. To find out how he's been doing. How his family was. Why he never wrote back or got in touch. *Didn't he want the same?*

Usually, taking on a heavy workload of courses was an easy way to stay focused, but everything felt muted and off.

By Friday, I was more than ready for the weekend.

"I think you should sleep over so we can have brunch tomorrow. You know how good the school's breakfast buffet is," Ava said as we turned the final bend, entering the vast hallway that separated the main academic buildings from the living quarters. "Oh, and the library will be right across the courtyard. So if you needed it, ya know."

"Sounds great. It's only our first week, and I feel like I'm already falling behind," I complained.

"That's because you're an overachiever and get in your head too much," Ava quipped. "Speaking of what's going on in your head. You talk to Beck yet? So weird he'd be here, right? I mean, talk about a crazy blast from the past. And so random," she rambled. But her words weren't lost on me. I asked myself the same questions. Yet, still haven't found a way to talk with him.

"Well, maybe he's scared," Ava continued.

"Scared? To talk to me?"

She shrugged. "You seem to be. Maybe he is, too."

"There's something not right. Ridgecrest is very selective in admission, and Beck should have graduated this past May." I sighed.

We continued walking, passing through the large common room. Filled with comfortable chairs, study tables, grand fireplaces, and even a made-to-order juice bar. Several enthusiastic students, no doubt eager for upcoming weekend plans, gathered near a circle of vintage high-back chairs.

Four entries that led to the designated buildings for resident students were located around the room. We traveled down the one that led to Ava's building and then up some stairs to her room on the second floor.

"Do we want to order in or go out? Ooh, I heard about a new Taiwanese eatery we could try," Ava said excitedly. At the same time, she tossed her jacket and purse on her desk before she headed to her closet. "Do you have tennis tonight? We could go after."

I began changing out of my uniform and pulled a pair of shorts and an oversized sweater from my bag. "Yeah, practice ends at 8. Let's order in. I already feel drained from the week and still have tennis practice." I stretched my arms over my head, walking over to her.

"Fine by me. I'll take care of it."

"Thanks, Ava, you're the best!" I told her as I gave her a little squeeze around the shoulders.

She smiled and squeezed back.

"Now, to all of this homework before I have to walk over to the courts."

Thwack...Thwack. The rhythmic sound of the ball hit the racket, causing vibrating pulses to flow into my hand. My pent-up energy released a little more with every swing. A sweet relief from the mess inside my head.

Tennis was my way to escape. To find a way out from complex things I didn't want to deal with. When emotions got too heavy, it was easier to avoid. Focusing on tennis seemed to help.

However, it was getting harder to distract myself from the never-ending questioning that played on repeat—Was Beck mad at me? Why didn't he write back? Why was he here?

I was finishing my set when Tristan, Andrew, and some of their friends walked into the courts, warming up to play on the one next to me.

There were four outdoor courts and two inside, and he just so happened to play inside today, too. I was doubting how much that was a coincidence.

"Funny, I keep stumbling into you here," Tristan's deep timbre sounded as he moved closer to the sideline of my court.

I struck at my last ball and nodded to the attendant to power down the machine. Resting my racket against my abdomen, I glanced at him.

"Well, I do play for the school. I'm kind of here a lot," I said.

"I've noticed." He smiled.

"So it seems. I'm about to finish up. But I'll see you around, yeah?" I turned to head to the locker room, but Tristan caught my elbow and stopped me.

"Hang on." His hand moved to his face, rubbing at his chin thoughtfully. "You see, I have this dilemma that I think you may be able to help me with," —he flashed me a mischievous grin— "I've been trying ever so hard to get you out of my head, but you're still there and don't seem to be leaving. I'm not very patient; I'm the type of guy who goes for what he wants. And right now, that happens to be you. What if we made these little interactions a little more casual, away from school grounds?" He spoke with complete assurance, his smile never leaving his face. *This guy. Is he serious right now?*

I was a little caught off by his forwardness. But then again, this was Tristan Dufort. I'm sure he was used to getting what he wanted. Maybe something more forceful was needed.

"Well, that does sound like you have a problem. Because, unfortunately for you, I'm the kind of girl that isn't very interested right now." *Did I really just say that to him?*

I wasn't sure where my confidence to be so bold came from, but if the smirk on his face was any indication, he wasn't bothered by my response.

He chuckled, his gaze fixing on me. "You know, I've always liked butterflies. A butterfly is a fascinating creature, but it can be difficult to catch. I guess I'll have to learn how to fly with you, Butterfly," he promised.

Umm, what? *I am not equipped for this boy's games. Leave now, Alessia.*

I nodded and started to walk backward. "Right. I'm going to go."

Tristan also began to walk backward toward his court. "I'll be seeing you," he said, finally dropping his gaze.

As I began my way to the locker room, for the second time, I heard Andrew hiss at Tristan. "What are you doing?"

I was too far away to hear Tristan's response clearly, but I was almost certain I heard him say, "If you want to be the master of the game, you have to get in the game."

I wasn't sure what he meant by that, but I was not interested in playing games with Tristan.

I grabbed a quick shower and left the locker room, swinging my bag over my shoulder.

The sun sank below the horizon, and the shadows around me grew. Walking the campus grounds alone after my practices was common; it never caused concern, but something felt off.

Wind rustled the leaves, and tense feelings of dread gripped as a chill quivered down my spine.

I increased my pace.

Goosebumps pricked with the sensation someone was following me. The weight of it was heavy, causing the rhythm of my heart to beat faster. *Get it together, Alessia. Just get to the dorms.*

My eyes darted around the path as I moved quicker toward Ava's building. When I finally made it to the back stairwell of the dorms, I told myself I was simply tired, that my mind was playing tricks with the shadows.

Still anxious from my walk, I reached the second floor's landing, taking the stairs two at a time. Upon opening the door into the hall, I heard some heated voices coming from further down.

Not wanting to intrude, I concentrated on my feet and tried not to look in their direction. But as I arrived at Ava's bedroom door, I peeked over at the couple.

It was the new girl, Chelsea, and Beck.

Wait, what? Was Beck staying in the dorms? On the same floor as Ava? Does he know Chelsea?

My stunned body stood like an idiot holding the door knob.

Beck had his arms crossed, his jaw clenched, while Chelsea argued with him in a low whisper I couldn't make out. She was angry with him. *But why?*

They both glared at each other when she finished and parted ways. I watched Beck go even further down the hall and make a right. *Should I follow him?*

Allowing impulse to drive me, I turned to follow.

There was only one door at the end of another short entryway where he turned. Beck wasn't there.

Reaching for the handle, I hesitated. Then the door flew open, and a hand grabbed my arm and pulled me inside, shutting the door behind us.

Beck stood mere inches from me, his hand still holding my arm. I looked up, and the first thing I noticed was the addition to his height since I last saw him. At least 6" greater than my 5' 4" frame, maybe 7.

Shock coursed up and down my body from the sudden momentum of being pulled through the door. And that he was actually standing there. In front of me. I inhaled a deep breath and exhaled slowly. His hand let go, and he stepped back.

The room was dimly lit; only one lamp in the corner supplied the space with light. Enough that I could see a light stubble covering his face. Hair disheveled and sweaty like he had been working out. His dark t-shirt also clung to his skin. It was more than his height that had changed; his whole body was more toned, with broad shoulders and a defined waist. He looked so grown up, not the boy I left.

"So you do remember me." I crossed my arms. Feelings of irritation rising to the surface. Blocking all other reasoning. "Care to explain what this is all about?" —I waved my hands

34

between us— "and while you're explaining, maybe throw in how you're at Ridgecrest?" I didn't expect to be so unpleasant towards him when we finally spoke. *I'm sure his avoidance has nothing to do with it.*

Beck quickly looked in my direction before his eyes diverted away, and I thought he might not answer. He didn't look happy to see me. *He's the one that dragged me in here.*

His hands went to his hips, and he sighed."Nice to see you too, Alessia." His voice had changed. He still sounded like Beck but in a more gruff tone.

Brown eyes glanced everywhere but at me. I tapped my foot, waiting for him to divulge more information. Beck and I used to share everything; I knew him, and he knew me. But that wasn't the case anymore. I had to remember we weren't friends like that now. And that hurt way more than I wanted it to. *Ugh, why is he so frustrating?*

"I know you have questions, but I can't answer them. Things aren't as simple as they look, and nothing is by accident with this school." His eyes finally found mine. "Don't trust anyone."

I watched him—eyes are often the most telling, revealing more truth than the words that leave our lips. He was hiding something. Beck always struggled to lie to me.

"That's it? You've been avoiding me all week. Acting like we didn't have years of friendship. And that's all you have to say? What does that even mean?"

His head shook in response. "Still so stubborn," he whispered.

With an unexpected bout of movement, he came closer. So close I felt every inch of his presence. I straightened, startled by his sudden proximity.

I may have been upset with him, but his nearness made my stomach do funny flips. *Stop, you let go of those feelings long ago, and he clearly does not have them for you.*

His head leaned in even closer, next to my ear. "You followed me, remember?" he whispered. "I need you to not do that. I need you to act as if we were never friends." His head pulled back, his gaze cast down. Reaching behind me, he grabbed the doorknob and opened it. "It's time to go."

I stared at his face. The face that brought back so many wonderful memories. He was stunning in all the right ways. But he was kicking me out.

I backed up through the door. Hurt. Angry.

"Why did you even bother to pull me in here?" I asked, some of the hurt slipping into my voice.

Beck looked at me then, the way he always did after Mom died, like I was something broken. "It was a moment of weakness," he sighed and shut the door.

Beck

I dropped my head and slammed my fist against the door, rattling it, foolish to think I could see her again. When I found her at the beach, I felt confident this would be an easy task. But that day in her history class, I knew my convictions would be tested. She was even more beautiful than I remembered. Her long hair fell down her back with soft curls, her hazel eyes capturing me. The shock and thrill that played across her face when she saw me made it all that much harder. I was doomed. I wanted to be around her. Hear her laugh, be the reason she laughed. Being near her again put life within me, like being filled with oxygen after going without. But I didn't know how to protect her from me.

36

Chapter 4

The door slammed behind me when I returned to Ava's room. Crushed, like all the joy in me had been sucked out, never to be restored again. I was more than disappointed in that initial conversation with Beck.

Sliding down against the door, my hands covered my face, exasperated. "Ugghhh!"

Ava looked up from where she sat on her bed with her laptop. Both eyebrows raised. "Practice went that well, huh?" she smirked. Closing her laptop, she patted the spot on the bed next to her.

I lifted myself off the floor and traipsed over, plopping heavily onto the bed.

"Hey, what happened?" she said, rubbing her hand up and down my arm.

"It's Beck. He's here. Down the hall." —I made a sound of disgust— "So stupid!" My head fell into my hands with a loud groan.

Ava stopped rubbing. "Wait, you mean he's on this floor? You saw him? Did you talk to him?" Her enthusiasm grew greater with each question.

I turned my head in my hands and looked up at her. "I saw him. I followed him. And then he acted like it was the worst thing ever to see me again. He asked me to act like we've never been friends."

I sat up and pulled my leg onto the bed, tucking it under the other. "Ava, I think I've lost him. For good this time."

"What do you mean?"

"Well, before, it wasn't anyone's fault. I left, and he obviously couldn't follow me. Now... I dunno, it feels like rejection."

"How?"

"With the letters, it still felt like we were connected. But now... it's like confirming he doesn't care." I moved off the bed and began pacing.

"Well, he's here now." Ava shrugged. "Maybe this is a chance to fix things." Her voice held hope, but then she gently added, "Or maybe it's time to move on and let what was in the past remain in the past?"

I stopped pacing.

Removing the hair tie from my wrist, I began twirling it between my fingers.

I didn't expect to see him again, but he was still a part of me. And to have him around and not be in my life would be the worst kind of torment. *Say goodbye to Beck forever? Could I do that?*

What I thought we had and could have been were now a distant memory. Fairytales weren't real, I knew that, but Beck was something more, and that was hard to move on from.

"I don't know," I said, shaking my head. "I don't know anything right now." I put my hands on my head, grabbing my wrist and holding it. A long exhale released. "I need ice cream."

Ava bounced off the bed, grabbed her phone, and said, "Here for it. Let's go!"

☙❧

Monday morning came, and I sat with Dad at our kitchen table, having breakfast together. A rare occasion since he was usually at the school before me. But with his upcoming trip, his classes were already being covered while he prepared to leave.

"How did your first week go?" he asked.

I moved my fork around my plate. *How was my week? If he only knew.*

"It was good. It's going to be a demanding year. I have two papers due by the end of the month and a calculus exam at the end of next week. But it will be good to devote my time to classes. It will help me prepare for Yale and qualify for scholarships." *And distract me from other, more unpleasant things to think about.*

Dad knew all of this. It was our usual song and dance. We hadn't gone deeper than work and school subjects in a long time. So I didn't feel the need to share the other parts of my week.

Dad nodded and swallowed some food. "Good, that's very good. I'm glad to hear it." After taking a drink, he wiped his mouth and pushed his seat back, walking with his plate to the sink.

"Dad, how did you know Mom was the one you wanted to be with?" *Where did that come from?*

This was uncharted territory. I honestly couldn't remember the last time we talked about her. Never wanting to bring her up and cause him pain. Cause me pain. I assumed he felt the same.

Dad set his plate in the sink and slowly turned to face me. His hands went on either side of the counter behind him.

He stood, pondering, and then. "Your mother....gosh, she captivated me like no other." He ran his hand through his hair and moved to return to the table. "I met your mother when I was only 21. She was 18. We were so young. She showed up one day in my life, and I knew I would never find another soul like her." Dad reached over and laid his hand on mine. "I'd say it's a matter of—when you know, you know."

He smiled at me, a real, genuine smile. He looked happy, with a hint of sorrow lingering. I smiled back because it made me feel good to know Dad loved Mom so deeply. That years later, she still evoked an affectionate feeling in him.

"Why do you ask? Did someone finally charm the heart of my daughter?" He chuckled lightly.

"No, just curious, and I've been thinking about her." I gave him a half-truth. Seeing Beck had brought up a great deal of nostalgia.

He hummed and stood again. "Whoever this fortunate young man may be, I hope he deserves you, Lessy." He smiled again and turned to leave the room. "If you need anything before you head out, I'll be upstairs packing."

I sat at the table a little longer, mulling over what he'd said. The advice wasn't exactly helpful for my situation. Beck was acting like a butthead. My best option was to stay focused on my academics and do as Beck asked—avoid following him or being his friend. No matter how much that hurt. *This is going to be so hard.*

Maybe we had found something extraordinary at one point, but I was no longer a naive little girl, and I could only hope that someday, someone could fill the hole he left.

I grabbed my school tote and left the house, choosing to walk again.

The breeze that skirted past my bare legs was much cooler than the other day. Autumn was calling, and it reminded me that change still held the potential for something beautiful in return.

Getting lost in my wandering thoughts must have slowed my pace because I heard the late bell ring as I hurried up the entrance steps. It didn't help that history class was the last place I wanted to start my day.

When I finally made it to first period, class had already begun, and Professor Gibbon was writing something on the board behind his desk.

"First and final warning, Miss Weber. Do try to be on time for my class," he said, glancing at me briefly as I walked by.

"Sorry, Mr. Gibbon."

I scurried to my usual seat in the back and attempted to squash any noise making. And keep my eyes from wanting to search out for a specific person. I failed.

He was slouched in his chair. The cap of a pen popping on and off in his right hand.

"Now, Mr. Dillard, you had a question about today's topic?" Professor Gibbon addressed one of the students in the front row.

"It's simple really. How can we know these secret societies play a role, when they keep everything they do so under wraps? How do we know that these significant changes in society throughout history have anything to do with these organizations?"

It took me a moment to connect with what he was asking. But then I remembered Gibbon mentioned on Friday that we would be discussing secret societies' role throughout world history.

"Secret societies often conceal their rituals, customs, and activities from the public. But that's the beauty of history. Everything leaves a footprint. Often times we don't see these footprints until we can look back and follow the trail. Hindsight, Mr. Dillard. This is exactly what I want to discuss today: How knowing mistakes from the past can help us avoid the same ones today."

I didn't mean to, but I tuned out the rest of the lecture. It wasn't normal for me to not be able to focus. Anymore, though, everywhere I went, and everything I did kept reminding me of my life before Ridgecrest. For some reason, that had me on edge about Dad leaving for his trip this week.

There was a scraping sound, and I realized students were moving from their seats and leaving class. I quickly gathered my items from my desk and threw them into my bag, following the crowd out the door.

Tristan walked up beside me as I exited the class. "Butterfly, have you been hiding? I've been looking for you. If it's me you're hiding from, what do you say we talk about how to fix that over dinner?"

I gave him a side glance. "We don't have anything to fix, Tristan. I've been busy, and if I recall, I believe I told you I wasn't interested."

He chuckled and put his arm around my shoulders. "Is that what you said? I heard something entirely different, Butterfly." *Of course, he did.*

I moved out from under his arm and stopped walking.

"Look, I think now just isn't a good time for me. You seem like a great guy, and I'm flattered. But I don't see it working right now." I grinned and started to move again. The truth was, Tristan and I were too different, and I wasn't sure I was ready for what he was asking.

His hand went to my shoulder to stop me. Turning to see what he wanted, his hand lay flat in front of me as if asking for something. "Daring." His eyes heated amorously. "You may know how to play the game better than you think. How about you give a guy a chance? Phone. Please." He wiggled his fingers back and forth.

I raised an eyebrow, taking in his impressive face. His smooth skin opposite to Beck's rougher facial details—the little prickle of hairs rubbing against my cheek the last time I saw him. *Stop! Get it together, Alessia.*

I knew I shouldn't use him as a distraction, but that's what I wanted. I was tired of Beck taking up so much real estate in my head. Plus, Tristan didn't actually like me. It was the chase. The thrill of the challenge. Nobody would get hurt with a little bit of flirting. So I pulled my phone out and handed it to him. "Here."

He tapped a few times on it, then smoothly placed the phone back in my bag and walked away, brushing my arm when he past.

I stood there a moment, watching him. My head shook, wondering what I had gotten myself into.

Continuing to my next class, I noticed another figure at the end of the hall, standing with his foot against the wall.

He wasn't looking at me but at Tristan. His posture appeared relaxed at first glance, but as I observed him a little longer, I noticed his hand fisted at his pocket, and a flash of something crossed his face. Anger, maybe?

He then turned his gaze on me. I thought I knew Beck, but this wasn't the Beck I remembered. Something changed. Because Beck had never looked at me with such loathing before.

Chapter 5

On Thursday, I had Dad request a leave of absence from school for the day so I could ride with him to the airport. The drive was over an hour, and I wanted to squeeze in the extra time together.

He shared his flight agenda, and I updated him on tennis training. Still avoiding any mention that Beck was now attending Ridgecrest. Not sure why I kept withholding that information. It felt like if I did tell him, I would have to face all these other emotions we never talked about, and I didn't know how to do that.

Dad pulled the car next to the curb when we reached the terminal drop-off zone. He popped the trunk, and we both got out, moving to the back of the car. He lifted his suitcase, placed it on the ground, and pulled the retractable handle up.

My arms folded around him, embracing him in a hug.

"I'm going to miss you. A lot," I mumbled into his shoulder, saying goodbye.

"I'll be a quick video call away." He pulled me back to look at my face. "I swear, you look more and more like your mother every day." He smiled warmly and hugged me again.

A small tear ran down my cheek as I watched him wheel his suitcases to the entrance.

"Be safe! I love you." I waved a final goodbye before getting into the car's driver's side.

Overwhelming deja vu and fear crowded my senses as I drove away. I remembered a very similar farewell happening only seven years ago. *It's fine. Dad will be fine. I can do this.*

Halfway back home, it started to rain. Driving the interstate sucked, let alone when it was raining.

Needing gas, I took the next offramp to fill up. With the car parked at the pump, I set it to autofill and climbed back in. After shutting the door, my phone chimed.

Ava: wanna grab coffee at urban brew cafe?

Me: sure! but aren't u at school?

Ava: i skipped....shhh ;)

Me: ?? be there in a few

The pump clicked. I got out, closed the cap, and grabbed the receipt. Getting back in the car, I tossed my phone in the cup holder and started driving again.

Back on the highway just beyond the next three exits, I took Elm St.—which would take me to Urban Brew. I took a few turns and found a parking spot on the street.

The coffee shop was busy and vibrant, a stark contrast to the gloomy day outside. Scrumptious smells of coffee and fresh pastries filled the air. I walked through the plush cushioned seats and tables and spotted Ava chatting with Chelsea at one of the high tables next to a rain-splattered window.

"Hey!" I greeted.

"Alessia! Hey! Everything go okay with your dad?" Ava smiled at me, hopping off her seat to welcome me with a big hug.

"Yep, he's all set."

"Great! Oh, I want you to officially meet Chelsea." Ava grinned and fanned her hand toward the elegant figure sitting in the other seat. "Chelsea, meet my friend Alessia. She's the one I was telling you about," she expressed

45

excitedly and continued with her introduction. "Alessia, this is Chelsea Fairmont. We bumped into each other on my floor the other day, and the connection was instantaneous. Chelsea is fabulous!"

"The pleasure is all mine," Chelsea said and nodded toward me. Her voice was deep and cultured. She had a slight accent that was diverse, and I couldn't pinpoint it. Like she had grown up around various languages. Her demeanor poised and confident. She was a bit intimidating if I was being honest.

"So great to meet you. Hope you're enjoying your time so far here at Ridgecrest." I smiled and fiddled with my bag strap.

"It suffices. Switching schools for part of my senior year was not ideal, but Father was adamant I experience some American culture." She shrugged her shoulder.

"That sounds terrible. I would not survive switching schools. But I'm so delighted you're here. I promise to make your time here beyond phenomenal," Ava piped in with remarkable enthusiasm. She then grabbed my hand. "Hey, I have a fashion design session tonight. You want to stop by after practice?"

"Oh, I really need to go to the library tonight." Of course, my assignments weren't due for another week, it probably could wait, but when I was stressed keeping busy was the best way to avoid unwanted thoughts.

Ava's face showed disappointment but quickly brightened. "Chelsea was just saying the same. Maybe you two can study together," she offered.

I looked over to gauge Chelsea's response. She seemed pleased.

"Perfect," she purred.

46

I hesitated but then said, "Yeah, sure. Sounds like a good time." It didn't; something about Chelsea felt off, and I still wondered why she and Beck were arguing the other night.

Ava climbed back up on her seat, and I went to the counter to order a drink.

When I returned to join them, Ava grabbed my arm and let out a screech, lifting her phone into my view.

"Oh, my gosh! Look at this. They're saying there is a bad accident on the highway near the school exit. A semi's trailer fell over and blocked the whole road. That's insane."

A live news update streamed on her phone. The report said a massive car collision occurred due to the blockage. No news on the truck driver or how he lost control, and the number of casualties was unknown.

I gasped and placed a hand over my mouth. "No—that's awful. Wait. When did this happen?"

"Like 20 minutes ago. So sad. And all those people." Ava pulled her hand back, her gaze fixated on the screen.

It was terrifying and devastating. A tragedy. Even more frightening was if I hadn't stopped to meet Ava, I would have been a part of that accident.

A motorcycle roared to life outside the window, drawing my and Chelsea's attention. Chelsea then stood and grabbed her jacket from the back of her chair.

"A fortunate turn of events for you, Alessia," she said mysteriously.

"Wait, what?" My head turned from the bike, registering her comment.

She slung her Prada bag over her shoulder.

"Are you leaving?" I asked.

"We were about to finish. I'll see you lovely ladies later." She winked and sauntered toward the door.

"Did that seem odd to you?" I asked Ava.

"Hmm?" she hummed, still focused on her phone.

"Nothing. Never mind." I sipped on my coffee, feeling a sense of unease, and wondered if it had to do with my dad or something else.

෭෨

Later that evening, I had on-court training with Carly—who also played for the school. She showed no mercy in our match, and I felt every bit of our practice as I hiked from the athletic division to the main campus.

The large three-story building with five education wings, in addition to dorms, stood prominently before me. A beautiful courtyard divided the space between it and another three-story building: the school library.

I pushed open one side of the double front doors and sighed in relief. There was a sense of peace I always associated with the place. Books had a way of doing that—the worlds to visit, the different lives to live, the information to discover all did wonders for my mental stability.

All the buildings of Ridgecrest were built in the early 1800s, but the library was my favorite. Grand and enchanting, the structure held tall, lavish ceilings and rows upon rows of books, aligned neatly in the built-in shelves framed with impressive woodwork.

As I walked further through the main entrance, I took note of my surroundings. Considering the time of day, I wasn't surprised few students occupied the space. Chelsea was picking through some books on the shelves nearest to me. Andrew, his mass of black hair disheveled and out of order, sat with another boy at a table across the room from me. Aside from those three, it was just me and the librarian.

I moved to a table with chairs and placed my things down.

"Hey, I wondered when you'd show up." Chelsea came up to my table and set her books down.

"Oh, hey! Yeah, practice ran late. I almost didn't come, but these papers won't write themselves." I chuckled.

"So true," she replied.

We sat together at the table, each working on our own assignments. I considered bringing up Beck, but I didn't know how to without being obvious or weird. But then my phone vibrated on the table, and a message notification popped up on the screen.

Tristan: Miss me yet?

I couldn't help allowing a small smile. *He sure is persistent.*

I clicked the screen off and chose to ignore him. Seconds later, he messaged again.

Tristan: It might interest you to know that I have this stunningly gorgeous girl still lingering in my thoughts.

I rolled my eyes and snorted. Who was this guy? Sending cheesy text messages? This was different from the image of Tristan I had assumed.

Me: Still don't see how that's my problem.

Tristan: Oh, but you are the remedy.

Me: That's interesting because I'm pretty sure I saw you whispering in the ear of the brunette sitting next to you today at lunch. You two looked rather cozy. So maybe she can remedy your problem.

Since Tristan didn't seem to be going away anytime soon, I may have started watching him a little closer. A guy like Tristan had his options, an abundance of them. Dufort was an exceedingly prosperous family. The family name was highly notable among the other Ridgecrest students and the community.

Tristan: Charlotte? Daughter of a family friend. She isn't what I would call my type. The more important detail is...you were watching me. I guess I'm not the only one with a lingering problem.

Oh my gosh.

Warmth spread to my cheeks.

Me: Not sure that's relevant.

Me: I'm going to find a book I need. gtg

I quickly put my phone away, wishing I hadn't responded to his initial text. In need of a couple more sources for my paper, I got up to locate the reference section.

"Where we off to?" Chelsea asked, her voice startling me.

"Oh, just getting some more books." I smiled.

"Lovely. Could you grab one for me?" Slender fingers slid a piece of paper across the table.

"Yeah, I've got you," I said, picking up the paper. "Be back soon."

"No rush," she said and went back to her laptop.

On the paper, written in small letters, was the title of a book and the library location. The south wing, opposite to where we were. Starting there made the most sense, and then grabbing mine on the way back.

This section of the library was like its own separate part of the building. A double door led into a round room lined with bookshelves reaching to the base of another floor full of more books. Each row had a wooden ladder attached to the shelf. Wheeling it to where I needed to, I climbed, nearing the top to retrieve Chelsea's book.

Something thudded against the ground a few rows behind me. Impulsively, my head swiveled in that direction. Was someone else in here?

The tip of my tennis shoe met with smooth hardwood floor, taking the last step off the ladder's bottom rung. More faint thuds stopped me from turning back the way I came from. With each step toward the sound, my apprehension grew.

Fast footsteps skated past between the aisles of books. The blur of a white shirt caught my eyes before a door slammed shut. A moment later, the blaring sound of the fire alarm went off. *That's not good.*

I needed to get out and fast. The library was installed with a high-end fire suppression system that diluted the room's oxygen and emitted a CO_2 spray. If I wanted to leave this room alive, leaving right now was my only option.

Quickly moving, my eyes darted around, searching for a glowing exit sign. One was just a few rows down from where I stood. Confident I could make the distance in time, I pumped my legs, racing to the door.

But I soon realized I was too late.

Tightness formed in my lungs. I tried and tried to pull in more air. But it was like climbing a mountain, and the air was thinning. My feet slowed. *Keep moving, Alessia.*

The room swayed like waves rocking a boat. Was I still going the right direction? I reached for one of the bookends, missing, and landed hard on the floor.

Breathing came in short spurts. *Get up now!*

A roar filled my ears—my heart thundering against my chest. This was it. All of it ending on the library floor from a lack of oxygen. It certainly seemed like the easier way. To simply give in. Give up.

Pressure built, warning the last breath was near.

An arm wrapped around and under me, lifting me off the floor. The figure holding me blurring in and out of vision. I couldn't tell who it was, but we were moving quickly.

We stumbled, me almost sliding out of their grasp. I was pressed closer to their chest. The beat of their heart hammered fast against me. Movement began again.

And then.

Cool night air kissed my face, and sweet oxygen relieved my crying lungs. A deep gasp as if breaking through water. The arms holding me let go, setting me down on damp grass.

A fit of coughs assaulted my body, searching for more and more oxygen. Groaning, I rolled over to find the person who carried me out gone.

I slowly sat up to look around. No one.

Flashing lights and the sharp whistle from the alarm were still going off. The south wing exit put me on the back side of the library. From where I sat, I could see students on the other side crowding the courtyard, curious about the commotion.

Chelsea, the librarian, and a few others spotted me and walked in my direction.

"Are you okay? What happened? We heard the alarm, and the librarian said the south wing's alarm had been activated," Chelsea said.

"The fire department is almost here. Was anyone else in the room? Are you okay?" The librarian knelt down, examining me.

I shook my head. "I—I don't know. Someone carried me out. I don't know what happened."

Chelsea's face screwed up like she was experiencing something uncomfortable.

I shared with them all I could remember happening before the alarm and again when the fire department showed up. They checked my vitals and kept me until the medical team arrived. A few short tests later, I was released, and they told me I was fortunate no serious damage was done. And I had to agree with them—I was lucky to be alive.

Chapter 6

Dreary overcast left it feeling earlier than it was, and a bad night of sleep made me miss the alarm. The night before had been riddled with anxiousness. After the library incident, I went straight home, showered, and crawled into bed. Avoidance. It was how I dealt.

With a half-tucked uniform, I rushed out the door and hopped in the car. A couple minutes later, I pulled into the school parking lot. Water sloshing at my feet as I ran from the car to the cover of indoors. Chatter among students greeted me in the main hall. I wasn't as late as I thought.

Not slowing down, I jogged up the stairs and turned the corner to my history class. Beck was there, standing next to the windows as if waiting for someone. *Waiting for me?*

"We need to talk," he said quietly, scanning the area around us.

I adjusted the strap of my bag on my shoulder and raised my chin. "I think that sounds like a novel idea, Beck. You go first."

His lips bent into a frown. "Not here."

He reached to grab my arm, but the weight of another presence moved close behind me. Beck turned hard eyes on the person standing there.

"I suggest you find your way to class, Beasman; the late bell is about to ring. Run along now. You're not needed here." The deep rumble of Tristan's voice vibrated against my back. Of course it's him. *But why is he calling Beck Beasman?*

Beck crossed his arms."I don't recall needing your permission. I'm sure she's capable of speaking for herself." His eyes drifted to me again. I thought I noted concern, but he was too fast to return his focus on Tristan.

"Actually, I would like to ask him a few questions," I said.

Tristan rubbed his hand down my arm.

"Ask away then, Butterfly."

Beck rolled his eyes. This was getting us nowhere. The tension cut sharper than a knife, and these two were dropping some serious hate. *Did they know each other? What am I missing?*

Tristan wasn't going to leave, and Beck wouldn't give me anything valuable with him at my shoulder, so I finally dropped my gaze and turned to the boy behind me.

"Ya know what? It can wait. We're all going to be late for class." I lightly pushed at Tristan's chest to get him to move. He was still throwing death stares.

"Sure, whatever you say." He fixed his green eyes on me and brushed his fingers with mine, interlocking them. "I'll walk you to class." *We're holding hands now?*

Beck rushed ahead, leaving me feeling like I missed an opportunity.

I glanced at Tristan's hand holding mine and gently tugged mine away. Unbothered, he remained by my side, leaving me at the door to my class with a wink before leisurely strolling further down the hall.

Entering class, I noticed the seat next to Beck's just so happened to be open and decided to take full advantage.

"I thought I told you not to follow me," Beck whispered.

A light scoff broke my lips. "But you get to interrogate me in the hallway?"

"I also told you not to trust anyone. You can't seriously be interested in him, Lissa."

The nickname hurt a little.

"I don't really see how it's your concern. And you don't get to do that. You don't get to ask me to not be friends, act like I'm not here, and then call me Lissa. You said we needed to talk, so let—"

"Is there something you need to share with the class, Miss Weber?" Professor Gibbon interrupted.

"Sorry, Professor, no. Please continue." I straightened in my chair and leaned back with a huff.

Beck also shifted in his seat, causing him to move a little closer to me. Annoyance spiked over his crazy mood swings, but I couldn't deny a little spark of hope flared at his nearness.

History dragged on until Gibbon finished with an assignment and class dismissed.

Beck didn't wait for me. Before I could even form a sentence, he bolted out the door. *Guess we're not talking then.*

With a heavy sigh, I set off to my next class, determined to not let all the unanswered questions wreck my day.

Eventually, it was time for lunch, and Ava was waiting for me by the taco station. Her blonde hair was curled and neatly styled, her uniform accented with stylish bracelets.

"The spicier, the better. Yes, thank you," she said to the guy behind the counter, who handed her a plate with three perfectly aligned taco shells and a side of guac and salsa.

"Hey," I said, grabbing a plate too.

"Hey," she replied, licking some salsa from her pinky. "You doing okay? You haven't responded to any of my texts."

"Sorry, just, it's been a day."

She nodded. "After last night, you ain't kidding. So, who do you think it was?"

I assumed she was referring to the person who helped me out of the library last night.

We stopped and grabbed a dessert before heading toward our usual table.

"I wish I knew. Maybe the person I heard leave came back?" I shrugged.

"Did you hear the announcement they gave about the fire this morning? Supposedly, the south wing is closed for investigation, and they're unsure how it even started."

We set our plates down. Esme and Tate are already sitting at the table but too engrossed in each other to even notice us.

Ava turned to me, a sparkle in her eye. "You know what I think? I think it was intentional. Like a real mystery to solve."

"Ava." I side-eyed her.

She scooted closer to me. "Hear me out. Everyone knows how intense that system is. No one is going to be dumb enough to just accidentally set it off or play a prank. So why then?" Her eyebrow lifted.

I shook my head and took a bite. The crunch of the shell breaking was my only response. Then reached for my laptop to squeeze in some time on my English paper.

"I heard there was no fire," Tate said. Fueling Ava's curiosity. I, on the other hand, would much rather forget the whole thing, even though a tiny part of me still itched to know who helped me.

"And we all know how we can trust the gossip ring," I said with a roll of my eyes.

"Shh." Ava waved her hand at me, encouraging Tate to continue.

"Some are saying they saw that new student and Andrew Fenton both leaving the south wing last night. Andrew's well known for his shady business deals. Probably a deal gone bad." Tate grabbed a fry, putting it in his mouth.

Ava leaned forward onto her elbows. "New student? As in Beck?" She faced me, lips parted.

Tate grabbed some more fries and shook his head. "Nah, the girl. What's her name—"

"Chelsea?" Ava asked, confusion crossing her features. "I thought Chelsea sent you there? Why would she go then, too?"

"I don't know, Ava."

Ava's questions of suspicion were inventing crazy ideas in my head. Beck kept telling me not to trust anyone. And every time I was around Chelsea, I got this weird feeling. Like she begrudged being near me. Another mystery to add to the pile.

Ava finished with her blueberry parfait and slid her dishes to the center of the table. "Come on, you're not the least bit curious?" she asked skeptically. "If there was no fire, then why the alarm? And you must be dying to know who your knight and shining armor is, right?"

"Maybe a little. But we don't even know if the rumors are true. Someone else was in that room. Maybe they started the fire."

"See! So then that still leaves the question of why."

I held her stare a moment."What I do know is, I have class in ten minutes." I stood and gathered my things.

Tate and Esme got up and left holding hands while Ava hurried to catch up with me.

"I'm pretty sure the library has cameras. We should go there tonight and see if we can look at the footage." A thrill laced her words, and I gave her a reluctant smile.

"Fine. I have a late practice, but we can meet there after."

"Yes!" She did a little hop.

Leave it to Ava to push my limits on my comfort zone.

෧൳

The sky was dark as I ran through the rain to the gymnasium for my evening training. All my efforts to avoid getting wet proving vain.

Concentrated on the wet hair in my face, I ran straight into someone. Two strong hands grabbed onto my arms, steadying me. "I am so sorry," I said, pushing at my hair.

I looked up, only to come into contact with the richest brown eyes. Eyes I knew. Eyes that somehow kept captivating me. "Beck!"

His hands still on my arms, I started to pull away, but he tightened his grip and moved us further into the shadows near the wall.

Rain dripped and plinked against the metal roof. Heavy breaths passed between us. Thump thump went my heart. Without permission, my body leaned closer. *Mmm, why did he smell so good? Ugh, we need to let go, remember?*

His forehead dropped, touching mine, and he sighed. "I don't know if I can do this," he muttered, pained.

"Beck? What *are* you doing? Why are you here?" I whispered. Meaning more than just here in front of the gym.

"I don't...," he breathed, sending a shiver through me. *Probably from the wet clothes, right?* "This isn't what I wanted to happen."

"What? Beck, you aren't making any sense. None of this is. Just talk to me."

He moved away from me in one rapid movement, taking his warmth with him. His expression torn, and then he was gone, walking away into the rain. *What is going on with him? And how am I ever going to escape this allure he had on me?*

His figure continued to retreat, and I wrapped my arms around myself. Frustration bled to concern.

"Beck," I yelled.

No response.

His behavior was erratic. Nonsensical. Not the Beck I remembered.

I walked through the doors and went straight to the locker rooms to change.

Arms stretched over my head, I stepped onto the court, ready to be pulled into the adrenaline release practice always provided—only to be met with disappointment.

Anxiousness surged, bombarding my attention, leaving zero focus except for a distinct encounter with a boy playing tricks with my emotions.

Questions bounced around, fighting to be heard. *Is he in some kind of trouble? What is his real reason for being here? How am I going to get him to talk to me?*

When did simple life become so complex? I didn't like it or know what to do about it.

Practice ended more frustrated and confused than it began. I wanted a reprieve from the mess in my head, not to get lost in it.

I showered and found myself alone in the locker room to finish changing. The last two girls left only moments ago.

It felt dark and eerie. Alone. The kind of feeling that brings about goosebumps.

I moved quickly to get dressed and tossed my hair up. The squeak of the door opening crawled under my skin. My head whipped around. *Did one of them forget something?*

I didn't see anyone.

"Hello?" I spoke into the emptiness. I swear I heard someone come in. *Eerie feeling increasing. Time to go.*

I turned back to grab my bag.

A sudden force from behind pushed me hard into the lockers, slamming my head against the metal. Whatever happened next, I wasn't sure because I couldn't help but fall into dark oblivion.

Chapter 7

*A*t the end of our property line, where our yard met the woods, sat the treehouse Dad had built for me the summer I turned 8. The space quickly became the go-to hangout for Beck and me. We would spend hours laughing over comics; Beck's were always the best, usually about some superhero beating the bad guy. We also had a secret compartment that hid all our favorite candy and treats.

Beck's house was only four houses down from mine—he was probably walking this way soon.

When I reached the top of the ladder, Beck was already there. Waiting. The clear Christmas lights hanging above were on, and he was sitting on one of the large floor pillows.

"Hey," I said, stumbling a little as I stepped onto the landing. He turned toward me at my fumbling and smiled.

"Careful, we don't need another broken arm."

I shook my head. He was talking about when he broke his arm from failing at a bike trick. I had to help him carry his books to class every day for months. I didn't mind, though. I liked Beck. I liked being around him.

"Unlike you, I'm quicker on my feet," I teased back.

I plopped onto the other pillow and nuzzled in, creating the perfect form for comfort.

"I can't believe you went and watched that movie without me," he said. But I knew he was just picking at me. He'd been doing that a lot lately, I noticed.

"Not my fault someone was too busy to go with me." I shoved his shoulder, and he fell half off his cushion laughing.

The pillow under me jostled as I crossed my legs, hands landing on my lap. "So you said you wanted to talk?"

He glanced at me, exhaled, and said, "Yeah, I do. Geez. Where do I even start?"

His hands clasped together, resting them on his knees. He seemed to be working up his nerve to say something. Drop some heavy news.

"I know I haven't been around as much as I used to, but I was hoping it wouldn't change things between us." His gaze held so much hope.

"Why would it?" I thought it was a silly question. Beck and I would always be friends.

Beck quickly became on edge. He sat straighter and slowly said, "There's been some changes in my life, and I don't know how to tell you everything. I also don't want to lie to you, Alessia. But can you trust me and know that there are some family things you are probably better off not being involved in?"

The way he was looking at me said it would mean the world to him if I accepted this vague offer and didn't try to press deeper.

The pillows we sat on were only about a foot away from each other. I leaned closer. There were hints of his shampoo and laundry detergent and something that just reminded me of Beck.

"Well, what can you tell me?"

Beck leaned a little closer, too.

"I can tell you that you're my best friend, and I still want you in my life."

His words did something to my insides. I felt elated and a little bit timid. I didn't remember feeling this way about him before. And I was suddenly concerned if he talked to other girls like this.

This fall would be my 15th birthday, and in the past year or two, I'd been feeling this way more often around him. Yes, our relationship had changed some over the past couple of years, but it was more than him being distant. My thoughts about him had shifted.

I no longer saw him as my goofy friend. I found myself wanting to be close to him. This giddy feeling exploded inside me when he was near, like a big happy smile in my belly. And I noticed things about him I didn't before, like how cute his hair looked when he let it grow a little longer. Or how intense his eyes were and made me feel like I was something special to him.

He bumped my knee and laid back on his pillow, looking up at the skylight. I crawled over to lay next to him.

Several hours went by of us gazing at the bright, sparkling gems in the sky. Bouts of laughter poured out of me with Beck's stories about his brothers.

The evening grew dark, and my eyelids were heavy. I curled tighter to his side, one hand on his chest. The beat of his heart increased. And an arm wrapped around me. Immovable. Safe.

Just before I fell asleep, the soft brush of his lips touched the top of my forehead. And a gentle whisper, "I will always be yours, Alessia," caressed my cheek.

Chapter 8

I sat up with a start. The urge to lie back down strong. My hands went to my head. *What happened? Where was I?*

The space around me looked like a bedroom. Cream curtains rested closed at the window next to the bed. A soft, plush comforter lay on my lap. *I'm in my room.*

Movement caught my eye, and I found Ava lying next to me. *How did I get here? Did I dream of someone attacking me? No, it was real. But that's crazy. Who would attack me?*

I checked the clock sitting on my nightstand. It was 3:30 in the morning.

Ava looked so peaceful, but I needed some answers. I nudged her shoulder. It did nothing, so I whispered her name, "Ava."

Another nudge to her shoulder. "Ava," I said a little louder. She finally blinked and turned her head toward me. A squeal erupted, and her arms wrapped around my neck.

"Gah," I winced out of her reach.

She pulled back, her hands going to her lips.

"Sorry! I was so excited to see you awake, and okay, I didn't think. How are you feeling?"

"My head hurts. What happened? How did I get here? The last thing I remember was being in the locker room after tennis."

Ava nodded, cleared her throat, and readjusted to sitting on her knees.

"When you never showed up at the library, I got worried. You weren't answering any of my texts either. I went to the gym first, even though it was pretty late. But you weren't there. So then I was really freaking out cause it's not like you to forget. Was about to head over to your house when Tristan texted me. Told me to check on you. He said you were found in the girl's locker room passed out. Must have slipped on the wet floor."

"That explains why my head is throbbing. Wait, Tristan? Was he there?"

"Uh, I don't think. He didn't say. He just said I needed to come to your house and check on you. When I got here, you were already in your bed."

Something wasn't adding up. "How did I get here? I don't remember walking home. Did he say who found me?"

She shrugged.

A fresh wave of memories consumed me—a door creaking, hands grabbing me. Walls started closing in around me. My heart was fighting to break free from my ribcage.

"Alessia. Alessia." Ava placed a few fingers on my chin and directed my attention to her. "What's wrong?"

My head shook. "I remember my head hitting the lockers. I don't think I just slipped. Ava, I think someone attacked me."

"Attacked? What? Tristan said you slipped."

"Was he there? How would he know?"

"I dunno. You should text him and ask. Yes, I think you should definitely do that," she said, smiling and bobbing her head up and down.

"It's three in the morning. He's probably sleeping."

"Yeah, but he's Tristan Dufort. He can totally help us solve all these mysteries. Maybe he was there or talked to whoever was and knows who helped you home. Plus the gymnasium has cameras too. Not in the locker rooms, obviously, but I bet we can see who is coming in and out."

I crawled out from under the covers and off the bed, searching for my phone. "I don't know where my phone is."

A heavy weight crept into my chest. The kind of weight that made everything feel out of control. *Inhale. Breathe, Alessia, breathe.*

"I'm sure it's here somewhere."

I slid my hands against my temples, brushing my hair back. "I have no idea what happened to me. I don't think it was just a slip. I almost died in the library the other night. And now my phone is missing." I sighed, tears forming. It wasn't just the phone; although I did want to find that, I was overwhelmed. There were so many unanswered questions circling my life. Beck showing up, and now all these weird accidents. *When would it end?*

"Hey, it's going to be okay," Ava said, hopping off the bed to hug me. "Here, I'll text Tristan to tell him you want to talk, and for right now, we can just go back to bed and figure this all out tomorrow. Okay?"

Sleep did sound better than thinking. "Yeah....okay."

When I finally staggered down the stairs much later in the day, it was almost 2 p.m. *Crap. How did I sleep so late?*

Yummy food smells were coming from the kitchen. I found Ava fixing a plate with bagels, avocados, and eggs.

"Morning, sunshine! I made you some breakfast. Or should I say lunch? I don't know, might even be too late for that." She laughed.

"Skipping classes two days in a row, Ava?"

"Boy, you really did hit your head hard. It's an Educators Training day—there is no school." She chuckled some more.

"Oh, right."

Rays of sunshine cascaded through the windows in the kitchen nook. Sitting down at the table, I closed my eyes and basked in the warmth on my cheeks.

"Here's your phone. I found it charging over there." She nodded to the other side of the kitchen.

"Gosh, I was such a mess last night." I took the phone and plate of food from her. "Thank you."

I tapped in the passcode on my phone, unlocking it, and read the few unread messages from Ava, and one from Tristan this morning.

Ava: hey, im at the library. where are u?

Ava: you should totally be done by now

Ava: there better be a fantastic reason you are not here yet

Poor Ava.

Tristan: Good morning. I invited Ava to stay the night with you. Hope that was okay. Didn't think you should wake up alone. She said you wanted to talk. I'll stop by later today.

Leaves blew across the ground at the same moment I glanced out at the backyard.

What was I going to do about Tristan? His attempts were becoming more genuine, and I wasn't expecting this sweet side of him. Was he really a nice guy? *Maybe you would know if you got to know him. Yeah, that sounded like a terrible idea.*

Worry over Tristan could wait. I reached for my phone again to call Dad. It went straight to his voicemail. *He's surely landed by now.*

I sent a quick text telling him to call me as soon as possible.

Ava joined me at the table with her own plate of food.

"Hey,"—she rubbed the top of my hand—"how you doing?"

"Dad's phone went straight to voicemail."

"Maybe he forgot to charge it. You know how your dad can be with his work."

"I sent him a text. I just hope he calls soon." I rubbed my hands up and down my face and winced. A pretty bad bruise was forming above my left eye. I released a long exhale. "What am I going to do, Ava? I'm feeling a little freaked out. I don't think I can stay by myself. Not now."

"Stay with me. Or I can stay here with you."

I bit my lip, considering her offer. Staying with Ava would mean I would be near Beck. That was both appealing and daunting at the same time. I kept telling myself I was letting go, but so much of me wanted to be near him. Know him again. Laugh again. Feel safe with him again. Those didn't seem like options anymore. But, on the other hand, staying with her would mean I'm not alone.

"That would be great. Let's stay here this weekend, and we can stay on campus during the week." I smiled warmly at her.

We finished eating, and while cleaning the kitchen, there was a knock at the door. Walking over to the entryway, I opened the door to Tristan's smiling face.

"Even with a knock to the head, you still take my breath away," he said. His hand clutching his chest.

I knew he was stopping by; he said as much, but him in my house was surreal. The image didn't fit right. And him out of school uniform and in dark jeans with a suede jacket was like seeing a fish out of water. Although a very handsome fish.

I motioned for him to come in. The oversized hoodie I was wearing fell down my extended arm.

"Thanks for coming," I said.

"Like it was a burden?" He smirked. "How are you feeling?"

"My head isn't hurting quite as much. Tired."

He placed his hands on my shoulders and examined my eyes. "Yeah, my doctor said some bruising and soreness would be expected, but he didn't expect the blow to have permanent damage. Lots of comfort and rest were his recommendations." He straightened and looked around the room.

"Your doctor?" I asked.

"Yeah, I called our family's private physician on your behalf. Explained to him what happened."

"And what exactly was that?"

His brows furrowed. "You slipped in the locker room, hitting your head on the floor."

I grabbed his hand and pulled him to one of the sofas. "See, that's what Ava said, too. But....I remember hands grabbing me and pushing me against the lockers. I don't believe it was just a slip on a wet floor or whatever."

Ava sat down on the recliner across from us, listening intently.

"You're saying someone came in and attacked you?" he asked. One corner of his lip crept up.

"Exactly." I eyed him. The half smile turned to a frown.

"I wanted to talk to you to see if you knew anything more? Like, maybe how I got home?" I asked, eager for more information.

He paused, his gaze passing from me to Ava and back. "You don't know?"

I shook my head.

"How did you know she was here?" Ava inquired.

Another pause.

"It was because I helped," he said.

"You did? So you were there?" I asked, a little stunned by his response.

"I wasn't there. My friend Andrew called me. He was leaving late from the gym. He said a janitor found a girl unconscious in the girl's locker room. When he discovered it was you, he knew I'd want to know about it."

I moved my leg up on the cushion I was sitting on and raised my hands. "Wait. You brought me home? Here to my house? How did you get in?"

He leaned back, taking a more relaxed position. "I'm Tristan Dufort." He winked. "Plus, your home is owned by the school. The Director has access to the lock codes."

"Then you told the Director what happened?" I asked.

"I told him what I thought had been the case last night. But if you think something else might have happened, we should inform him. He'll be able to look at the footage to see if anyone followed you there."

"That's what I said," Ava shouted.

Tristan's head nodded, and he leaned forward again, pulling his phone out.

"Then I'll get something set up." He started typing on his phone. "Your father left for a long trip, yeah?" He glanced up at me before returning to typing.

"Yeah. How did you kno—"

"I'm in his class. If you were attacked, you shouldn't be staying alone." He pocketed his phone and returned his focus to me.

"I'm staying with her," Ava said, getting up and walking toward the kitchen.

"I was thinking something a little more invulnerable," he said loudly to her back.

She turned. Mouth open in mock offense. "Hey!"

71

"What were you thinking?" I interjected before Ava actually did become offended.

"I would stay with you," he said plainly.

I blinked. "Oh."

No, I was not okay with that. I barely knew him.

"I think if Ava and I stay on campus grounds, that should work out," I continued.

Tristan was undeterred. "If that's what you would prefer, that could be a temporary solution. Until you feel more at ease with mine."

I smiled to appease him and didn't say any more.

It sounded like he went the extra mile to see that I was cared for. But that had me disconcerted. I was grateful for all his help; it was sweet and caring and surprised me. I didn't expect such attentiveness from him. *What am I supposed to do with that?*

Tristan stood. "I need to get going. I have family obligations," he drawled.

He reached down and pulled me up by the hand. "I think last night revealed to me what I was missing. I hope you can forgive my strong approach to gain your attention. It was a bit much. Tends to come with the territory of being a Dufort. I'll do my best to not be so much."

Doesn't like the word no is more like it.

"No worries," I said instead.

We walked to the door and said goodbye. Ava came up behind me, a glass of water in hand.

"Full steam ahead, girl. I don't know what you are waiting on," she said and walked over to turn on the TV. "Movie or series?" Ava offered.

I walked over and joined her on the couch. "Series."

For the rest of the evening, we watched Gilmore Girls and ordered takeout.

Distracting was my first line of defense. Curling in a ball and wishing it all away sounded like a great plan of action.

Chapter 9

Every call to Dad landed me in his voicemail throughout the weekend. It wasn't until Sunday morning I received a text from him.

Apparently, after getting his luggage, he fell down a crowded escalator, injuring his back and left leg. He claimed he was fine, and it would take him a few weeks to heal enough to put weight on his leg again. He would stay in a hospital in Yokohama, Japan, during the healing time.

News like that only pushed me further on edge, and I blasted his phone with text messages asking a bunch of questions about it. His only response was a "call soon."

Early Monday morning, he finally video-called me.

"Oh, Dad," I said. Sympathetic for his position—he was lying on a hospital bed with several pillows behind him. "How are you doing?"

"The amount of pain meds they have me on, I'm feeling quite fine." He chuckled. "How are things at home? You said you needed to talk. Everything okay?"

I debated how much I wanted to tell him. Realistically, he couldn't do anything from his hospital bed in Japan. And I wanted to wait for actual evidence that someone did attack me before making him worry.

"Things are a little messy. I didn't like being alone, so I'm staying with Ava for now. But mostly, I just wanted to make sure you were okay." I forced a smile.

Dad sat up, adjusting the pillows behind him. "I'm sorry to hear that, Alessia. I was sure a little stint away would be no big deal for you. Do you need me to come home?"

I could hear the sincerity and regret in his voice. He wanted to be here. A small thrill jumped in me. Dad was choosing me over his work, but it wasn't good timing.

"No, of course not. Look at you. You're in a hospital bed with a banged-up leg."

His head nodded. "Well, that's true. They're telling me at least three weeks before they will release me. Let's see how you're doing then. I'm glad you have Ava."

"Yeah, me too." It was good I had Ava. Dad and I didn't have anyone outside the two of us. He was an only child, the same as Mom. And I never met his parents; both died when I was young. Mom never talked about her parents. Besides Dad, the Cirillo Family and Ava have been the closest family I have ever had. Until I lost the Cirillos, too. *It always comes back to Beck. Stop thinking about him.*

"You going to be okay?" he asked.

"Yeah. Yeah, it'll be fine. You focus on getting better. I'm not entirely alone. Plus, we plan to stay on campus in the dorms. So lots of people around."

Dad and I talked for a little longer. He shared about his flight and the little bit he had seen of Japan. We ended the call, and I felt a little better knowing Dad had landed and could be reached. It was awful he got hurt and was stuck in the hospital, but at least he was still breathing.

I hopped off Ava's bed and walked over to the closet where she was getting dressed.

"What am I going to do about this?" I dabbed at the bump on my forehead; the pain had weakened to a dull annoyance, and the bruising was a subtle black and blue.

75

Ava tossed a fashionable checkered scarf at me. It matched well with the black and gold colors of the uniform.

"Try that." She continued to rummage through her closet.

"I don't think I'll be able to get it low enough." I examined the scarf and tried tying it like a headband.

"Hmm, it'll be fine." She leaned over, adjusting the straps on her heels. Our uniform didn't require heels; the shoes just had to be black, but Ava would never miss a chance to show off her fashion sense.

"How fun is this? Getting ready together, sleeping over every night, late-night girl talks. It's like I finally have the sister I always wanted." Ava smiled brightly while applying her mascara.

I leaned into the mirror next to her, applying my own makeup. A little of her excitement growing in me."Yeah, it's like being a little kid again, excited for the next moment with your best friend."

Hearing that thought aloud rubbed harder than I expected. *I miss Beck.*

Why did things in life have to change? The excitement I just felt ebbed away as my mind drifted.

Routine was my friend. Without it, I felt out of control. Beck being here and acting all strange had me off kilter. Other things weren't helping much either: Like Chelsea and her crypticness, almost dying in the library, a bruise on my head clearly yelling things were way out of order. The imbalance hit too close to other moments when life was out of my control.

Grappling with so many mixed emotions weighed on me. I didn't like feeling helpless. It was an emotion I never wanted to face again, in the dark, not knowing how to move forward. But as it was, I did feel helpless, and all I could do was hope it didn't destroy me.

My phone pinged, notifying me of a new e-mail. It was from the school. They wanted to see me in the office. *Guess hiding away from it all is out.*

Ava and I grabbed the last of our things and headed to the academic wing. We parted ways at the grand staircase by the main entrance. Ava went to her Stewardship class while I continued to the Director's office.

An elegantly trimmed opening led into a room filled with several doors. Gold letters above it spelled out Administration Offices. A large desk was positioned just inside, and a woman with greying hair sat at it, typing.

"How may I help you?" the woman asked me.

"Alessia Weber, here to see Director Langley."

She looked up at me from her seat. Her petite nose barely held her glasses up.

"Do you have an appointment? I'm afraid his schedule is rather full this morning."

"Uh, I received an e-mail. Asking for me to stop in before classes."

"Miss Weber. I'm glad you're here. Please have a seat in my office." Director Langley spoke from his office door.

The secretary simply looked at me over her glasses and nodded in his direction as if to say, 'You heard him.'

I entered the Director's office and sat in one of the plush seats in front of his massive desk while he walked to the other side and stood sifting through some papers.

I fiddled with my hands, not entirely sure why I was there. The e-mail didn't mention why they wanted to see me.

"Miss Weber, it has come to my attention that you have concerns about a certain incident that happened to you Friday evening on school grounds? Is that correct?" Director Langley asked. *Oh, that's what this is about.*

"Yes, I do. I don't know exactly what happened, but what I was told and what I remembered aren't matching up."

He glanced up. "I see. Mr. Dufort seemed to agree with you that an investigation may be necessary." He straightened the papers he was looking at on his desk and took a seat.

"Is there new information then?"

"We've reviewed all the footage from the date in question and did find one instance that caused us to take a closer look at the timestamp of your entry into the locker rooms."

"You did?" Trepidation set my heart racing. A part of me was hoping I was wrong, and it was faulty memories.

"We asked that you come in today to help us identify the man we found entering the locker room 20 minutes after you entered." He angled his large computer screen toward me. The screen showed a split view of the hallway leading to the locker rooms at the gym. He pressed play, and a hooded form dressed in all black rushed through the door to the girl's one.

"The movements are quick, and it's hard to catch any distinct characteristics, but..." he backtracked the video and slowed down when the person in black first appeared on screen. Catching a slight profile of the figure. "Here is the only moment we can see any of his face. And we never see him leave. It's possible he crawled through a back window."

It was clearly a male, and anyone else looking at this would only be able to tell just that. But I knew this male. If I thought my heart was pounding before, it picked up another ten notches.

I don't know what it was about him that made me so aware of him, but I knew without a doubt that the person entering the locker room after me was Beck.

"Miss Weber? Do you have any ideas who this individual may be?"

I hesitated. Beck wouldn't hurt me. But why was he there?

"Sorry," I said, shaking my head. "I don't know who that could be."

He frowned at the screen and angled it back in place. "I'm sorry this wasn't helpful, Miss Weber. It is clear something more went on that night than we know. Being my job to protect Ridgecrest students, we will continue to look into this and keep you informed. With your father away, I would like to offer you a room on campus."

"Oh, I actually already am staying on campus. I'm staying with my friend, Ava. Ava Nomad. I think that should work for now. Is that all?" Things just became extremely muddled, and I wanted to leave before my emotions showed on my face.

"Also, we have a school counselor ready and available to talk with if you want to do so. It might be helpful to process with someone," he said.

Forgetting it happened and moving on would be a lot less painful at the moment. "I think I'm okay right now. If that changes, I will let you know."

"Alright then. If there is anything else, please feel free to contact the office." He handed me a slip of paper. "A tardy slip for your first period."

I took the piece of paper and stood. "Thank you, Director Langley. I appreciate all you're doing."

Swiftly leaving the Director's office, I walked down the empty halls to history class.

Doubts and scenarios of why Beck would be there flitted through my mind. My desire to understand why he was here escalated. I stumbled into class due to my thoughts being so preoccupied.

"Miss Weber, everything alright?" Professor Gibbon asked.

I looked over at him and then glanced at the rest of the room. Every eye was watching. I inwardly groaned.

"Yeah, sorry I'm late." I handed him my late slip. He nodded to indicate I should join the rest of the class.

I straightened and went to my seat in the back. Stopping halfway, I blinked a few times. Beck sat in the seat next to mine. I kept walking, scrutinizing him with suspicion. His body looked tired and taut.

I sat in my seat next to him, side-eyeing him. He exhaled, and his body relaxed considerably.

Professor Gibbon's voice rang out as he began his lecture and went over the weekend's homework, "Did anyone take me up on the extra credit and look into the recent passing of Michael Vasili of Vasili Inc.?"

Yeah, I was a little busy not dying myself. Didn't really get around to homework.

The itch to drag Beck out of here and make him talk to me was intense, but not wanting to draw more attention to myself, I grabbed a notebook and quietly tore a piece of paper out.

We really need to talk. And why are you sitting next to me?

I folded the paper and carefully slid it across to his desk. Just like we always did as kids.

He tapped his pen against his fingers but stopped when he saw the paper. He glanced at me. A hint of mirth crossed his features.

From my peripheral, I watched him unfold the paper and write something. When he passed it back, I noticed his knuckles were bruised and scabbed.

Butterflies fluttered in my stomach as I took the piece of paper and unfolded it. *No, we are not allowed to feel butterflies right now.*

I needed reassurance. Why were you late?

Reassurance? Reassurance for what? Why do you have bruises on your hand?

His posture stiffened as he read my response. Another quick scribble, and he passed it back.

Why were you late?

I had a meeting. Can we please talk after class?

He nodded and folded the paper, keeping it in his hand. *Is he not going to reply?*

I huffed and slouched in my seat, crossing my arms. He leaned back, too, and placed his hands in his pockets. *Stupid boy. He does wear his school uniform rather nicely, though. Ugh, no, he had things he needed to answer for.*

When class was finished, Beck quickly walked behind me. The barest contact nudging my jacket as his arm reached around me, dropping the folded piece of paper we were passing. Unfolding it, a winky face stared back at me.

What?

Butterflies melted and boiled into outrage. Beck was hiding things. I needed answers. Our current dance was torturing me.

I stuffed the paper in my bag and followed him. I was about to reach him through the crowded hallway when someone stepped into my line of sight.

"How's my beautiful girl today?"

"Tristan," I said, failing to keep the irritation off my face, and I think he noticed.

He turned to look behind him and then turned back to me with an inquiring stare.

"Everything okay?"

"Yeah. How are you?" I kept moving, not wanting to lose Beck; I didn't know where his next class was. Tristan followed along beside me.

"Better now. Walk you to your next class?" *How chivalrous of him.*

I looked around as Tristan continued talking, but I couldn't see Beck anymore. *Blasted, I lost him.*

"Alessia, did you hear me?"

I gave him my attention; he looked annoyed. "Sorry, I was looking for someone. What were you saying?"

"I asked if you cared to join me for lunch today."

"Uh, yeah, sure. Sounds great. Well, this is me,"—I leaned my body toward the classroom to emphasize—"see you later? Thanks for walking with me." I waved and entered my second period feeling deflated and more flustered than ever before.

Beck

Skipping my next class, I jogged down the stairs to find an empty room. My steps slowed as Tristan rounded the corner, facing me.

His hand rubbed at his jaw as he watched me.

"She likes you, you know? I can see it in the way she looks at you. The way her eyes always find you if you are in the same room. Certainly explains her resistance to me. I can't figure out why, though. How you effortlessly snuck in after I already had my hold." His eyes narrowed. "I don't trust you. You best watch your step, Beckett. Before someone gets hurt."

I laughed. Zero humor behind it. "The feeling is mutual. Don't worry. I'm here for one reason, and when I'm done, you won't see me again."

Leaving this place couldn't come soon enough. Especially done with this idiot and his games and watching him put his hands all over Alessia. I wanted to punch him in the face every time I heard him call her Butterfly. But I couldn't let those feelings interfere.

My plans were drastically changing. I should have known she would affect things. She always did. Always pulled me in. I was struggling more than I wanted to admit. Losing focus. I didn't lose control like this. But it was too late. It didn't matter, I'd make a new plan. *It will work. It has to work.*

Tristan rammed my shoulder as he went past. "I'm watching you, Beckett," he sneered. Then he voiced over his shoulder, "A word of advice. I'm not very fun to make enemies with."

I rolled my eyes and kept walking. Yeah, I was done playing things safe.

Chapter 10

"Then she said Brandon was caught cheating on Francesca with Melody." Charlotte Rees's pink lips turned up in a sly smile as she shared her juicy dirt about some girl's love life from her dance class.

When I agreed to join Tristan for lunch, I didn't think through what that would look like. We sat at his normal table with the rest of his circle of friends: Andrew Fenton, Everett Blair, Charlotte Rees, and his sister, Opal Dufort. I invited Ava to join us, but she said she would sit with Esme and Tate.

She didn't fail to share her enthusiasm about the prospect of Tristan and me, though. Even with me continually telling her I wasn't committing to anything.

I really wished she would have sat with me. I was out of my element. These kids came from old money. Blue bloods. Practically American royalty. Plus, Andrew, who sat next to me, kept glaring at me. *Total creeper.*

"Well then, we'll have to ensure Melody knows her place. Poor Francesca. I told her to leave that boy alone long before anything ever began. Who does he think he is messing around on her like that?" Opal said. Her appeals sounded anything but sorry for her friend Francesca.

The gossip continued between them while I kept quiet, enjoying a Thai basil steak sandwich.

"Not much for chatting today?" Tristan rested his arms against the table and focused on me.

"Umm, sorry." I shook my head as if to clear it of bad thoughts. "I have a lot on my mind lately."

"I imagine you do." He leaned in closer and whispered in my ear. "Listen, I had a meeting with the Director this morning. He showed me the video. I think--I don't trust that new student. I'm not saying it was him, but I want you to stay away from him. Something is just off."

I whipped my head in his direction at his words. Did he know it was Beck, too?

"Why do you say that?" Words tumbled out of my mouth, tripping over each other to be first.

He remained close to my ear. "I'm a good judge of people. And a girl I know said she saw someone that night who looks exactly like our little friend over there,"—he nodded toward a table where Beck sat—"lurking about the gymnasium." He leaned back in his chair, popping a grape in his mouth.

Beck and I ran into each other that night before I went into practice. Did he come back later? But Beck wouldn't attack me. *Would he?*

I glanced to my left and noticed we had piqued Andrew's interest. I scooted closer to Tristan.

"You sure? I saw him there before I started my practice. But the Director said no one had been identified yet."

He shifted to face me. Barely inches from each other, I'd be touching him with the smallest movement. *Not even the slightest tingle. What is up with that?*

"Humor me. Stay away from Beckett." His words seemed sincere and determined. Before I could question him further, Charlotte's voice broke into our conversation.

"Beckett? You know, there's something sexy about all that mystery. He's in my French class, and his pronunciation is flawless." Charlotte kissed the air with her fingers. *Flawless French? Beck doesn't know French, or at least he didn't.*

Tristan and I turned to look at her, eyebrows raised. She shrugged her shoulders. "You can't fault me for noticing him. All the girls have, trust me," she said with a little hum.

"That's because they've had to live with the same moronic idiots that fill our school and social gatherings every year. He's fresh meat. But he's insignificant. A pawn to be sacrificed. Someone to call when an itch needs scratching," Opal jeered, and she and Charlotte chuckled.

But I wasn't laughing. Slapping the smile off her face was the more appealing course of action.

I didn't know Opal, but she was proving to be exactly what you would expect from a self-entitled witch. How can she think she can give value to someone based on what they have to offer her? And she was talking about my Beck. *Wait, 'my Beck'?*

"Sounds like you've put a lot of thought into someone so insignificant, Opal. What do you know of this Beckett?" Andrew spat the name.

Opal frowned. "I said he is a toy to be thrown out. So why would I know anything about him?"

"Yeah, and I can't find anything on him online anywhere. I mean, who doesn't have TikTok," Charlotte added.

"There are ways to find out about people beyond their tweets and videos, Charlotte," Everett retorted, glancing up from his book to speak for the first time.

"I can think of a few better ways," Andrew chuckled and winked at the girls.

Losing interest in this conversation fast, I moved in my seat to grab my bag and leave when I caught sight of the table Beck was at. He stared in this direction, a severe frown formed on his lips. He caught me watching him and looked away. Tristan noted my attention, as well, and lightly touched my arm.

"Do you know him?"

"Hmm?" I responded distractedly. "Know who?"

"Beckett? The guy you were just giving eyes to across the room?"

That brought my attention back. "What? That's crazy. I wasn't giving eyes. I was curious. He's in my history class... and you did say you suspected him."

"Hmm, why don't we do something to help get your mind off some things. I'm having a yacht party this Saturday. How about you come?" he said, hitting me with one of his charming smiles.

"I don't know," I mumbled, searching my brain for a plausible excuse to not go. "Is that a good idea with how crazy my life has been lately?"

"I'll be there with you. You'll be fine." He pushed some hair behind my ear.

"Ooh, that's right, I nearly forgot that was this Saturday. Can I invite Beckett? Oh, I'd be the envy of the whole party!" Charlotte squealed and preened before the table.

"Ya know, including him would be a great idea," Tristan agreed. Andrew shifted, appearing more annoyed than before. Charlotte clapped joyfully while grinning at Opal, who rolled her eyes and took a bite of her food. All the while, Everett continued to be focused on his book.

"Really?" I asked, surprised.

He leaned in near my ear again. "Keeping our enemies closer, no?"

I pulled back to peer at him. His green eyes revealed his resolve, and his mouth lifted slightly in the corners. *He seriously thought this was a good idea...and saw Beck as an enemy. Was Beck my enemy?*

"Count me in. But I'd like to bring Ava," I conceded

"Terrific." Tristan beamed.

I slipped my bag back on the chair and pulled out my laptop. Tristan confirming what I already knew about Beck left a bad knot in my stomach. So I did what I always do when I didn't want to feel yucky things—avoided. Convincing myself that if I ignored the emotional storm long enough, the thunder and lightning would cease to exist. *Right?*

∞

When I informed Ava we were going to Tristan's yacht party, she was adamant we needed to outfit shop.

On Friday afternoon, we drove to Blush Boutique, the trendiest fashion store within the city limits.

After sifting through several clothes racks, we created a pile of potential options on the circular leather sofa in front of the dressing rooms.

Ava went first, picking a black top and matching bottom. A few minutes later, she flung the curtain open with flair and jutted her hip. She was killing it. The top was a slightly cropped halter paired with high-waisted flowy bottoms.

"What do you think? Tres chic?" She twisted back and forth in front of the mirrors.

"Yes! I love it. You look amazing!"

"I love it, too. But not for the party." She moved over to the pile, sifting through it. "I think I want the creme jumpsuit, yeah?" Her head twisted to look at me.

"Oh, yeah. That one will look good on you and show off your toned arms."

She did a little excited clap with her hands. "Be right back." She returned to the dressing room with the new outfit.

"Did you hear from your dad this week?" she asked.

"We talked a couple times. He can now have meetings in his hospital suite because they moved him to a bigger room."

"That's good." She came back out looking adorable in the strapless jumpsuit. "Look, it has pockets. And I have the perfect heels for this."

"So fun." I smiled.

"Okay! Your turn," she said, running over to the pile of clothes. She held up a sage high-waisted free flowing maxi skirt with a slit to above the knee, paired with a white scooped neck cropped tank top.

I stood to take the pieces from her. The material was soft and expensive.

"That is gorgeous. But do I need it? We already have so many options in the closet at home."

"Quit being so practical, Alessia. This is a Dufort family yacht party. We show up in style. No arguments. Now, try this on." She turned me around and shoved me toward the curtained room.

Closing the curtain, I lifted my shirt over my head.

"So things with Tristan seem to be moving along nicely," Ava commented from the other side of the curtain. There was curiosity in her voice; she wanted details.

Tristan made it his personal mission to be around me more. It made sense she would start to wonder. It wasn't anything serious, though. The right thing to do would be to tell him that, but it was easier to put it off. Delay. Make excuses.

"Harmless flirting and hanging out, Ava. It's no big deal. I mean, he surprised me a few times with sweet gestures, but he's not interested in something real. He'll move on soon enough." I pulled the curtain back and sashayed out.

Ava gasped. "Ahh, I love it! You have to wear that! Pleassse."

I turned to examine myself in the mirror. The outfit complimented my figure well, and the sage green skirt brightened my eyes, the slit adding an allure of sexiness to the whole thing.

"Tristan will be tripping over himself when he sees you tomorrow."

The problem was Tristan wasn't who I was hoping noticed.

Chapter 11

Attending Ridgecrest Academy meant you carried a certain status. A status that allotted a world of opportunities and avenues to people of influence. Students who attended such a school would never be known for anything less than an elaborate party.

Tristan's party was on a three-level yacht with a pool, DJ, catered food, face painting, and even a magician. *Am I going on a cruise, or to a high school party?*

Apprehension built as we arrived at the docks. Beck was going to be there. He had been extra elusive all week. Missing classes and avoiding me like I had a disease.

The boy had me all over the place. I wanted to talk to him, but also wanted to hit him. *How did he go from wanting to talk to completely ignoring me again?*

Tristan was convinced he was dangerous for me to be around. But Beck didn't act like he was the one who hurt me in the locker rooms. He passed notes with me in class. That's not dangerous. Beck wasn't a danger to me.

At least not physically.

With Beck, I cared too much. It was all the little things. He inflamed so many emotions in me that I thought I might explode. Even with all the good and bad, it didn't matter. No matter where I was in life, he would always have a piece of my heart, a piece that smiled every time I thought of him.

When we were little, we would laugh so hard I couldn't breathe. The way he held my hand when we jumped from the pier at Aberdeen Lake. How he always got a chocolate milkshake when I would get vanilla because he knew I struggled to pick between the two.

Just to look at him brings all those memories flooding back. Makes me think how amazing it would be to have that kind of friend again. The kind of friend that knows me. Really knows me.

And that was dangerous. To care so deeply about someone just to possibly lose them in the end. Absolutely terrifying.

Walking on the yacht, music boomed across the main deck. Vibrations from the bass coursed through me while the sun on the cusp of sinking below the horizon reflected brightly off the water. People were everywhere, filling the opulent space. The main deck appeared to be the fullest, with dancing, games in the pool, or feasting on the impressive buffet.

Ava and I weaved across the dance floor to the beat of Cake by the Ocean by DNCE. She grabbed my hand and moved us closer to the inner part of the deck. An island food bar sat in the middle of the room, offering hors d'oeuvres and drinks. We grabbed some before seeking a more relaxed place to sit. In the back of the room was an open door leading to the next deck level.

Reaching the top of the stairs, we found Tristan, Andrew, and Opal sitting on some sofas in the middle of the deck. Tristan stood to greet us, his rolled sleeves drawing my attention. He did look particularly attractive in his casual white shorts and an unbuttoned navy shirt.

"Welcome, ladies. I was beginning to worry you wouldn't show." He pouted his lip.

"Alessia's not usually one to not follow through with her word. No need to worry," Ava chirped.

A devilish smile graced his face, and he waved his arm toward the sofas.

Accepting his invitation, we walked over to join them. Opal was sprawled out in a green bikini with a sheer covering loosely tied at her waist, so Ava and I chose the one next to hers. Andrew scoffed, stood, and walked into the cabin.

That awkward feeling when it felt like you just walked in on something you shouldn't have laid thick around us, and we all started talking about the weather. *So awkward.*

A more sensual beat dropped on the dance floor. I swung my head in that direction, spotting Charlotte moving in rhythm against a shirtless Beck, who rested his hands on her hips. My stomach dropped, and I felt sick—wanting to look away but unable. Like the worst kind of car wreck: too horrifying to watch but too transfixed not to. Finally, the song changed, and Charlotte grabbed his hand, leading him inside.

"I need a bathroom. Where do I find one?" I asked Tristan.

"I can show you." He began to rise, but I stopped him.

"No." Throwing my hands up to stop him. "I mean, really, it's okay. Just point me in the direction?" My attempted smile fell flat. I didn't feel like smiling. More like sitting on the floor and crying.

"Inside. Head to the doors toward the bow. It will be the first one on the left." He jerked his thumb over his shoulder.

"Thank you." I quickly moved out of my seat, eyes narrowed on my feet. But a sharp bout of laughter hit my ears as I reached the doors to the inner sanctuary I desperately wanted.

Charlotte and Beck came up the steps to the same deck I was very much also on. I don't know why I didn't just continue on my merry way and enter the cabin.

I stood there. Frozen.

Beck's eyes met mine as they passed. His laughter and smile gone. Warm eyes roamed over me, a rigidness took hold of his jaw, and his lips narrowed. He was silent as they joined the others. *Oh, my dear heart, why him?*

I whipped the door open and quickly closed it behind me. This room was smaller than the one below, and the lights were off. I navigated to the front of the room and located the bathroom.

Turning on the sink, I splashed my face with water and told myself there was never a Beck and me. To pull myself together. I was being stupid.

Once I collected myself, ready to return to the deck, I grabbed the door and was about to open it but stopped. Voices were coming from the other side.

"Don't tell me to calm down. If things go south, it will be because of that asshole—he's screwing everything up! The library? Everything would have gone down that night if not for the shit he pulled. Where did he come from? I knew getting this Verndari Order involved was stupid from the start," Andrew's angry voice drifted into the bathroom. *The library? What's a Verndari Order?*

"Does it matter at this point? You guys are in too deep; there's no climbing out. You need to get it together before people start asking questions. They don't know who's behind it. Beckett's here; whatever part he thinks he plays is inconsequential. And stay clear of him before he does something more than a bloody lip and a black eye. I don't trust him. You do your part and see the deal through." Another voice said, but I couldn't make out who.

"Yeah, right, he puts hands on me again. I'm taking him out...."

Their voices grew distant, like they were walking away. Making a small crack in the door, I checked to see if they were gone—the room was empty. *What did they mean about seeing the deal through? Beck, what are you involved in?*

I went to find Ava, but she was no longer on the couches outside. The others were still sitting and talking, but the conversation abruptly stopped as I sat down next to Tristan.

Suffocating tension crept across my skin. Beck looked out at the water while Charlotte laid her long legs over his lap, snapping selfies. And Andrew looked on the verge of murdering someone.

My hand brushed Tristan's leg as I twisted to face him. "Sorry. Do you know where Ava went?"

He looked down at my hand and smiled before he brought his eyes level with mine.

"I believe she said something about grabbing drinks with Chelsea before hitting the dance floor. Care to join her?" he said, offering his hand and glancing at Beck. Impulse drew my attention to look, too. Beck shifted, knocking Charlotte's legs off, but his eyes never made contact.

"Yeah, why not." I placed my hand in his, and we stood together.

At the bottom of the stairs, I once again was hit with a rhythmic bass vibrating through every inch of me. Tristan spun me into his chest, and his hands found my waist. He swayed us to the beat, leading us into the moving and bouncing crowd, completely lost in the enthralling sounds that teased our ears and bodies.

I allowed the music to consume me, to let it take me to another place. Where I wasn't concerned about Beck and how I lost him. To a place where strange things on campus were no longer a thought. Where I could just be in the moment. The crowd sang along to the lyrics, and I sang with them. Letting the music take control of every part of me.

I don't know how long we danced, but lights around the pool and cabin flickered to life, and the space around us became dark.

Tristan leaned next to my ear. "I'll be right back. Keep dancing."

I nodded and moved closer to Ava and Chelsea. The beat moving my hips.

Feather light tickles fell down my arm as someone moved next to me. I turned my head to see who and found myself absorbed in a pair of very familiar chocolate colored eyes. *Beck found his shirt, good for him.*

I kept dancing, challenging him to join me. He matched my movements and drew close, so close to touching but not, and I somehow felt him everywhere. He grabbed my hand and placed a cup in it.

"You looked thirsty," he said.

His gaze transfixed on me as we swayed. Hypnotizing beats faded the world around us to where it was just me and him.

I lifted the cup to my lips, drawing his eyes with it, and felt the cool liquid reach my tongue and venture down my throat.

The music pulled us even closer.

His arm snaked around my waist, finally closing the distance entirely, connecting our bodies.

Colliding.

Bonding.

Creating an emotional avalanche, like pieces falling together. Like the last piece of the puzzle. Complete.

Leaning closer, his face brushed into my hair. My eyes shut, and I breathed him in.

How could it feel so right to be held by a boy who seemed to hate me?

"Why won't you tell me what's going on?" I whispered against his chest.

"You don't know what you're asking," he whispered back with a sigh.

"I know you're hiding things, Beck. You shouldn't even be in school anymore." I leaned my head back to look up at him.

He stiffened. Then, abruptly, he pulled away, tearing us from the moment. And I watched him walk away toward the pool where Opal and Charlotte sat soaking their feet in the water.

Ava moved to my side.

"What was that about?" she yelled, competing with the music.

Hurt and anger rushed in like dark, heavy rain clouds. Tears pricked.

"I need off this boat. Like, right now," I said and shoved my way through the crowd to the side of the yacht, dumping the remaining contents of my cup into the swirling water below. *I don't understand these games he's playing.*

I continued my trek to find the ramp to the dock and entered the lower-level cabin. A shiver shook me, and I rubbed my hands along my bare arms. The cabin lights were bright coming from the dark outer deck, and people were everywhere.

I pushed past someone when a wave of dizziness swayed me. Stumbling to find the wall, my hand reached out to brace myself. My other hand rested on my head until the reeling had subsided. *That was weird.*

Regaining my footing, I walked to the other side of the room. Hot, sticky bodies jostled me, but I still shivered. An even stronger wave of vertigo hit me. About to collapse on the floor someone reached out and caught me. I tried to place the individual, but the room wouldn't stop spinning. More chills came. Intense pains of nausea with it. *What was happening to me?*

My eyes fell shut. The person who caught me was carrying me back outside because when my eyes finally opened, the sky above was dark, and tiny stars twinkled back at me. Nausea squirmed again inside me, and a groan escaped through my lips as I wiggled to free myself from their hold.

"I think she's sick," a male voice said above me.

The person holding me laid me down on something soft.

"Let me through! Idiot." A female voice drew close. "Alessia, sweetie. It's Ava. Can you hear me?"

Ava? Oh, Ava, help me, please. I feel like I'm dying.

The words were stuck; they wouldn't come out. My body twisted, and the only sound that left me were more moans. Head still spinning, I was sure I would be throwing up all over the place at any moment.

"What's going on?" Tristan's commanding demand entered the mix of chaos around me. A hand gently touched my head and swept my hair back.

"She's not responding to me. I don't know. She looks to be in a lot of pain! Hudson had her, said she was falling over." Ava's frantic hands swept over me. "Alessia, listen, you're going to be okay. I'll get you help."

I tried to nod, but my body lurched as my stomach endured more pangs.

More moaning.

It felt like my insides were eating me alive. I just wanted the pain to stop. I screamed and writhed. Larger and firmer hands brushed my face.

"Alessia, I'm going to take you to the hospital," Tristan said. "Hello? Yes, get me a helicopter to the docks. Don't even think about questioning me."

Everything was discombobulated and fading in and out, but I could feel hands on me, moving me from the yacht to firm land. I last remembered hearing a heavy door slam and Tristan yelling, "St. John's Hospital, now!"

Chapter 12

Tristan carried me out of the helicopter and rushed us across the roof. Attendants waited for us at the door on the other side.

My focus was blurred. Every time I attempted to figure out what was happening around me, a wave of dizziness caused my head to fall against Tristan's chest again.

"What are her symptoms?" a female nurse asked as they placed me on a gurney.

"She's conscious but non-responsive. My best guess is abdominal pain. She was twisting and moaning while holding that area," Tristan responded, his earlier assertiveness gone.

"Miss, can you hear me? My name is Claudia. Can you tell me how you are feeling?" The nurse, Claudia, leaned toward me. "We need to get her into medical imaging; we'll need a CT scan and an MRI. Then we'll get her set up for blood work," she said, speaking to someone on my other side.

I groaned some more, incoherent words leaving me. "My stomach...so much pain. Dizzy...everything...." I leaned over and retched all over the floor.

The nurse nodded and continued to rattle instructions off to the other nurse as they pushed me down the hospital hallway.

After several body and head scans and endless blood work, I was placed in a private room with an IV and heart monitor. This seemed serious.

I dozed off and on between a few more puking spells. My body was tired, but I could feel the stomach cramping beginning to subside, and I could open my eyes without the room spinning.

"Ah, you're awake this time." Tristan strolled into my room with some flowers in a vase. "How are you feeling?" He placed the vase on a stand next to my bed. "Also, Ava said you needed something to brighten your room."

"Thank you. Uh, getting there. Still tired. My head hurts, but my stomach no longer wants to be outside me instead of inside." I chuckled, attempting some light humor.

Tristan smiled. "Happy to hear it. You had us all in a real panic." He grabbed my hand and began rubbing the top of it with his thumb. "The doctor has reports he wants to share with you. Should I tell him you're awake? Or would you like to rest some more?" *Wow, that was incredibly thoughtful of him. Maybe I have been wrong about Tristan.*

"I'm good, thank you. I'd like to see him."

He pressed a button on the side of my bed. Then got up and picked up one of the chairs by the window and placed it next to me.

"What time is it?" I yawned.

"Almost 3 in the morning." He stretched his arms above his head and yawned, too.

"Geez, how long did I sleep?"

"Several hours. I left to make sure Ava made it back to the dorms. She was determined to stay, but I assumed you would sleep through the night, so I told her I would update her if anything changed."

"But you are going to stay all night? In a hospital? For a girl, you hardly know?" I said, a dubious look apparent on my face.

He leaned back, feigning offense. "You cut me, Alessia." Then, a charming smile. "As a matter of fact, I am planning to stay. I couldn't leave you here alone."

I felt a small twinge of guilt at his words. It wasn't supposed to get serious. But his being here, wanting to stay here, felt serious. I wondered if I should say something. Put a pause on wherever he thought this was going. But at that moment, the door opened, and a nurse came in.

"Hello there, could you let Dr. Pullar know Alessia is awake?" Tristan informed him.

The nurse nodded and walked back out.

Tristan brought his gaze back to me. "Need anything? Some water? Food? Whatever you would like."

I stared at him. My feelings of guilt and people pleasing warring within. "Water would be great, thanks," I said.

Tristan walked to a small table across from the bed and poured water from a pitcher into one of the cups. As he returned to my side, the door opened again, and Dr. Pullar came in.

"Miss Weber, so good to see you awake. How are we doing?"

"Better," I chirped.

The doctor's face looked pleased. "Good, that's very good. Considering." His shift in tone set me on edge. He was looking at his clipboard and nodding as he spoke.

"Considering what?" I asked.

He moved the clipboard lower and gazed in my direction. "Considering the traces of white baneberry we found in your system. You were fortunate it was such a small amount. With higher levels of the toxic berry, it is likely this conversation would not be taking place," he said solemnly.

Tristan tensed beside me.

What was he saying? That I should be dead right now? "White baneberry? What's that?" I asked.

"It is a highly toxic plant. Its berries can be deathly. If too much of the poisonous berry is consumed, it could cause cardiac arrest or respiratory paralysis. There's no telling if you would have made it to us in time if that were the case. Any ideas about how you came to eat the berry? Mr. Dufort informed me you were all at a yacht party. I assume you didn't accidentally pick it off a bush." *Poisoned? I was poisoned?*

My head began spinning again, but not from the poison. I could have died. That was now the third time my life had been physically threatened in the past two weeks.

"No, I don't remember eating any berries or anything that even looked like a berry." I leaned back against the bed, replaying my day in my head. *When did I eat a berry?*

"I can assure you there would have been nothing like that at the party. Could it have happened before she came?" Tristan asked.

"The toxins are relatively quick to take effect. How soon was she showing symptoms after arriving at the party?" Dr. Pullar asked.

"It was...It was after dancing. I was leaving, and I got really dizzy. Someone caught me, and then the stomach pain." I looked to the doctor.

"Hmm. Did you have anything to eat or drink at the party?" He asked.

"I told you that would be impossible. My family screens and checks all hired staff before an event." Tristan released a frustrated breath.

The doctor's eyes widened, and he gave an apologetic nod.

"I am merely asking questions. It's not common to see someone with baneberry in their system that didn't happen upon it during a hike or the like. What about the party guests? Have any others reported being sick? I can check if we have had any other cases, but to my knowledge, Miss Alessia is the only case we have seen tonight."

I reflected on the evening, trying to remember what I might have eaten or drank. And then it hit me. *No, it couldn't be that.*

"Um, I did have a drink while dancing." I hesitated, not wanting to face the truth of what this could mean.

Tristan's attention fastened on me.

"I don't know what it was. Or where it came from." My cheeks warmed. Party code 101: watch your drink.

"When? I was with you." Tristan's features twisted with incredulity and annoyance.

"After you left, someone brought me a drink and said I looked thirsty." I shrugged my shoulders, playing it off as innocent. But I knew who gave me the drink. Both Tristan and I knew of my recent attack and who was suspect number one. What would he think if I shared who?

I returned my gaze back to the doctor. "Do you think it could have been in my drink?" *Please say no. Please say no.*

"I suppose it's possible juices from the berries could have been added to a drink. But it's highly unlikely someone procured enough berries to actually make a decent amount for drinking," he said.

That can't be right. No, because that would mean...

The beat of my heart kicked up in speed, and my thoughts whizzed around, bouncing into each other so fast I didn't know which one to concentrate on first. *Was my drink really poisoned? Why would Beck want me dead? Why would anyone want me dead? None of this was making any sense.*

My emotions must have been evident on my face. Tristan's hand grasped mine, resting them together on the bed. I zeroed in on the heat of his hand, trying desperately to find something stable to ground my racing suspicions.

"I'll look into this evening's intakes and let you collect your thoughts. Perhaps there are other possibilities you are forgetting." Dr. Pullar placed the clipboard on my door and left.

"Alessia," Tristan said into the quiet. "Do you know who gave you the drink? You said someone."

I hesitated again, fiddling with the hem of the blanket. "We don't know it was the drink." I inwardly winced. Because a big part of me knew that made the most sense.

He gave me an incredulous look. "Alessia, you know what this looks like. No one else at the party got sick, and it was not brought in through catering accidentally. Who gave you the drink?" His tone grew low and sharp like a knife.

I closed my eyes and breathed in, hating where this conversation was going. "Beckett," I said on exhale.

I finally allowed the word to leave my lips. I opened my eyes and peeked at Tristan. He was staring at me with a look in his eyes I couldn't identify—part rage but part confusion.

"I know what you're going to say. But why would he try to kill me if it even was the drink?" Failing to keep the panic from my voice. My chest tightened in an attempt to will the tears from coming.

This looked bad. So bad.

But even if it wasn't Beck, someone was trying to take my life. *But why?*

"I haven't figured that out yet, but he was at the gym, and now this. That's strike two. We'll need to take extra precautions from here on out, and I'm having Beck brought in to the Director for questioning." He gave me a pointed look, telling me he wouldn't accept any objection.

As I thought back on all his strange behavior: asking me to pretend like I didn't know him, playing cold then hot, always disappearing but showing up randomly. The conversation I overheard on the yacht popped into my mind. *The library? Everything would have gone down that night if not for the shit he pulled.* Beck was at the library. Did he pull the alarm?

Then he was acting strange outside the gymnasium before the attack in the locker rooms. And last night, he may have poisoned my drink. *That's three strikes, Beck. What is going on with you?*

I noticed my phone sitting on the stand next to my bed. I reached for it and saw several missed calls from my dad.

"Did the hospital contact my dad?"

Tristan looked up from his own phone. "I believe so, yes."

Oh, Dad. He was probably so worried.

"I need to call him."

Tristan nodded and stood. He moved the chair back next to the window and sat, propping his feet on the chair across from him. His eyes shut, and his head leaned back. My own body felt tired and weak, but a quick call to Dad and then I would rest.

"Hello? Alessia? What's going on?" He answered frantically after the second ring.

"Hey, Dad. I'm guessing you heard I was in the hospital?" I started running my hands up and down the blanket.

"They said you were fine but had been poisoned by some kind of berry? How did this happen? Is someone with you? Is Ava with you? I never should have left. And now I'm stuck in this damn hospital bed on the other side of the world."

"Dad, it's going to be okay. I'm already starting to feel better. I should have known better than to drink some mystery drink at a party. Just a crazy accident, ya know." I'm not sure if my words eased his concern. They certainly didn't ease mine. Dad and I knew too well how quickly an accident can change the course of life.

"And I'm not alone. Ava was here, but she went home to rest. My friend Tristan is staying, though."

Dad sighed. "Oh, Lessy. No, it's not okay. I've failed you. Again."

He looked away from the screen, and a long silence followed. I shifted in the bed, unsure what to say.

"How about...you tell me how you're doing?" I asked lightly

Another sigh. "Still a long path of healing. My back is killing me unless I'm on the medication they have for me. My leg isn't as bad." He paused, looking away again. "It's been nice being able to visit the outdoor spaces in a wheelchair. They have some of the most stunning gardens I have ever seen." He continued to share about the city's beauty and sights around his hospital. I smiled as I listened. What else could I do? The alternative was too hard. It's funny how frightening moments can pull us apart, but depending on our response also have the power to bring us closer. With Dad, it always seemed to build walls.

"Alright, I'm going to get some more sleep. I'll talk to you again soon?" I said.

"I would love that. And, Alessia...I love you."

"I love you too, Dad."

The call ended, and I tried to go back to sleep, but my brain was still on full alert. The idea that someone may be trying to hurt me wouldn't let go. Unable to deduce why anyone would want or need me dead. And I couldn't escape the nagging coincidence all this started when Beck arrived. It made it hard to convince myself that it was just a coincidence. *What if it wasn't? Could Beck betray our friendship like that?*

He distanced himself before I moved and never replied to any of the letters I sent him. It wasn't unrealistic to think his feelings had changed. But was he really here to end my life?

Chapter 13

The hospital released me late the next day. My body felt fine, like nothing ever happened. I wondered if I hadn't dumped the remains of my cup and instead drank more of it if that would be the case. *Did he intend for me to drink the whole thing? No, Beck wouldn't poison me.*

The idea Beck would want to hurt me was a reach, making the idea of him trying to kill me beyond absurd. But the odds were stacked against him, and I didn't know how to fight against that kind of evidence.

Dad and Dr. Pullar agreed with my theory that it was a party prank and that I should have been more careful with what I was drinking. I believe it was only to appease me, though. Tristan, on the other hand, did not trust Beck. He also knew Beck was the one who gave me the drink. His suspicions would not be as easily swayed.

Tristan pulled into the school's parking lot, where Ava waited for me at the main entrance to the residential wing.

"I have some things I need to take care of. You'll be okay with Ava?" Tristan said.

I nodded. "Yeah, honestly, I feel so much better today."

"Are you sure you wouldn't rather stay with me?"

"I'll be fine with Ava." I chuckled. "Thank you for giving me a ride home."

I got out and waved goodbye.

Approaching Ava, she gave me a big squeeze. "You had me so scared," she mumbled, tightening her hands against my shoulders.

"I know. But I'm okay." The quake in my voice couldn't be hidden. I wasn't okay.

"Alessia." Ava frowned, and tears shone in her eyes.

"It's fine. Let's go upstairs."

Once in Ava's room, I showered and changed into leggings and a hoodie. I then filled her in on what the doctor discovered and our suspicions of how it happened.

"Okay, I get you guys were friends before, but you were so young then. And he sounds kind of dangerous. This could be for the better, ya know. Tristan, on the other hand..." She sighed dreamily. I also told her about the conversation I overheard at the party. Didn't do any favors for her feelings toward Beck.

"I don't see it, Ava. What would his motive be? We haven't even talked in three years."

"Ooh, remember how Tate mentioned a deal going down at the library with Andrew back when that all happened? What if Beck was part of that, too, and Tate was right, and something went south? If they found out you were there too, maybe they think you overheard something. And people do crazy things to cover the bad things they do. Trust me, my dad's a lawyer. You wouldn't believe some of the cases he's had."

"Ava, you watch too many suspense movies. That was Tate's theory. What if Beck's the mystery guy who helped me in the library?" My chin jutted upward, indignant.

"Then why poison you? You need to be careful around him. You've never been knocked out in the locker rooms before he started coming here, either." Her eyebrow went up, and she tilted her head.

I sighed and pressed play on our next movie choice. "Let's get lost in Chris Hemsworth's sexy voice and stop talking about this. Please?"

The opening score played on the screen, and Ava's hand pressed against mine. "You will be careful, right? I mean, you've always had this part of you that's, I don't know, hidden. But lately, you've really pulled inward. I'm here to talk if you need to." Her green eyes entreated me.

"I'll be careful, Ava."

Monday brought a new week, and I planned to continue to do life, pretending everything would sort itself out. Eventually. Even though I knew that's not how things worked. Within the two weeks since school started, I wondered if I could go to the bathroom without someone jumping me. *Maybe it's easier to not think about it.*

My ambitions to go to university and begin my path following my mother as a college professor felt silly compared to the worries that now tormented me. How could so much change so fast? *Well, that's a stupid question, Alessia. You know it takes only a second for everything to change.*

Turned out that adjusting back into my routine was far from easy. My class work was sloppy, and I was slow at my practices, missing easy strategy points and losing momentum with my swing.

Coach agreed to only schedule me for sessions during other teammate training times, so I was never alone while at the gymnasium. That did little to ease my tension.

Tuesday afternoon, I had on-court training again with Carly.

Walking onto the courts, I saw her holding a racket and bouncing a ball on the opposite side of the net from me.

"Ready to sweat, Weber?" Carly hollered across the court. "Ready to get out of my head," I yelled back.

Immersing myself in training and assignments wasn't helping me avoid the looming storm of fear, angst, and doubt thundering inside of me. Usually, it was easier to be in denial than to face life and death realities. My realities were getting harder to deny, though.

Thwack. I hit the ball hard, running to catch Carly's return.

I was no stranger to dealing with death, but it was different when it loomed over me, threatening to take me, any moment, at the hand of another.

Thwack.

And it hurt worse to think this person was Beck. Were all the events leading up to the poisoning connected? Elaborate schemes to end my life? No, I was too deep in my head. Too many scary shows creating farfetched ideas. Why would someone be trying to kill me?

Thwack...thwack.

I stopped, breathing hard, and began pacing around the court. Walking out the energy, bringing my heart rate back down.

"You doing okay there, Weber?" Carly walked over to my side of the court.

I continued panting. My hands rested on my hips. Giving her a side glance, I nodded and went back to pacing.

"Alright, well, good match. You need me to stick around till you're ready?"

I nodded again. "Yeah...I'll be in...just a bit," I said through labored breaths.

I bent over, placing my hands on my knees, attempting to clear my head. It didn't help that I started having recurring nightmares. Endless scenes of fires and someone chasing me, each ending with Beck and I dancing before he knocked me unconscious.

And I was being careful. I didn't go looking for Beck, and I hadn't seen him since the party. If I could just get him out of my head, I might make some progress.

Carly and I entered the locker rooms, grabbing quick showers before walking back to the dorms.

Reaching Ava's room, I opened the door and tossed my duffel on the floor. I started messing with my still wet hair, twisting it into a hair tie.

A white dress box sat on the bed, catching my attention. Taped to the box was an envelope with my name in fancy lettering. Ava entered the room as I continued to stare at it.

"Hey!" she said, flinging her jacket on the chair by the desk. "What's that?"

"Haven't opened it yet." I ripped off the envelope and pulled out the heavy square piece of paper.

Dear Alessia,

I cordially invite you to my family's annual benefit ball

Friday evening

On the 22nd of September

At 7:00 pm

I wanted to treat you to something special to wear, so I had my mom's designer pick this out for you.

Hoping you will be my date,

Tristan

Dropping the letter on the bed, I removed the lid of the box. Inside was a beautiful champagne gown. My fingers grasped the delicate material by the thin floral detailed straps and lifted the floor length masterpiece, admiring how the pattern of flowers continued through to the v-neck bodice and branched off like weeping willow wisps into the flowing tulle bottom. It was breathtaking.

"Wow! That is—that gown is gorgeous," Ava breathed. "Ooh, I have the perfect shoes for that." She bounced off the bed and into her closet. I folded the dress back over itself and placed it in the box.

"See. Wait, what are you doing?" she asked.

"Putting it away."

"No! We have to put it on. When is the benefit?" She picked up the letter. "It's Friday? Oh, so much to do. I'll call Maria's and get you in for the full set - hair, nails, and makeup. Eeek, this is so exciting!" She moved to the top of the bed, sitting while she called someone on her phone.

I laid the dress against my chest, swishing it around my feet, as I watched myself in the mirror across the room, unsure what to do. How to respond to such a gesture.

Tristan's feelings were growing for me, and I couldn't say the same in return. Persistence and kindness toward me made it hard to say no, though. I didn't plan for this kind of involvement. I would meet his parents and be at his side during a high society function. This was well beyond harmless flirting. This required letting Tristan in. Required vulnerability. *Was I ready for that?*

I grabbed my phone from my bag to text him.

Me: Love the dress! It's beautiful. Thank you!

Three small dots popped up immediately.

Tristan: Is that a yes?

My finger tapped the side of the phone, hesitating.

Me: It's a yes.

Tristan: I'll pick you up at 6:30

I let out a heavy exhale. This was good. Setting aside fears and trying something new. *Yes, I could do this.*

After modeling the dress and finding a complimentary hairstyle, we hung the dress on the back of the closet door and ordered takeout. We ate together on the floor when it arrived, laughing at stupid memes Ava found on her phone. Our laughter died down as she searched for another one.

"I noticed you haven't been sleeping well," she said, continuing to scroll through her phone, her eyes darting between me and the screen. "Everything okay? Do you want to talk about it?"

I knew this moment was coming. The nightmares I'd been having woke me with screaming. Ava never stirred, but I had doubts that she wasn't noticing.

"It's just some bad dreams." I was going for casual, even though the messiness of my life was anything but casual.

"And Beck? Has he said anything to you or tried to be around you?" She put her phone down, her apprehension evident.

"No. He's been MIA so far this week. I haven't seen him in history, at lunch, or even in the dorms."

"Really? Did Tristan have him questioned like he said?"

I went back to picking at my meal. "Yeah, Beck had plausible reasoning for every situation. At least enough that their small amount of evidence against him doesn't hold for further investigation." I shrugged. Tristan was furious when he told me. And then he increased his time around me. He probably would have wanted me out of Ava's room if he knew Beck was on her floor.

"Huh, that seems strange. Do you think he's sick? I think something may be going around because I haven't seen Chelsea all week, and when I texted her, she said she wasn't feeling well."

Was Beck sick? No, I didn't think Beck was sick. It felt like he was avoiding me. Again. Beck was staying away to hide something. He always struggled to lie to me. Whatever he was hiding, he didn't want me to find out.

Chapter 14

With my arm looped through Tristan's, he guided us up a short set of stairs. My heels silent as they pressed into the soft carpet that descended the length of the stairs. Tristan's body next to me kept the chill of the night at bay.

Long, curled tendrils of hair tickled the skin on my back and arms. With my free hand, I held my dress to avoid tripping as we reached the top of the stairs.

The Dufort's benefit was being held in the grandest mansion my eyes had ever seen. The night sky, speckled with twinkling stars, complemented the elegant floral displays and splendidly dressed guests. We entered the foyer, and more floral displays greeted us. Whites, purples, and greens. And above us hung an ostentatious crystal chandelier. Everything around me breathed luxury and refinement.

A man in a suit directed us into a large room off the side, much like a grand ballroom, filled with chandeliers, magnificent high-vase centerpieces, and even more elegant floral designs decorated the columns that lined the grandiose space.

We stopped at a table where a man and woman stood, greeting guests. The man looked exactly like an older version of Tristan, and I realized he must be his father. They shared the same firm jawline with a narrow nose and lush hair. Their expensive tuxedos even matched.

That must have meant the woman was his mother. Wearing a tasteful one-shouldered gown in a deep blue, her dark hair styled in a sleek French twist, pulling the outfit together with pearl accessories.

"Tristan, my dear. I'm so glad you are here." His mother embraced him and kissed his cheek, forcing me to step back.

"Mother, you've outdone yourself, as always." His eyes scanned the room.

She touched her chest. "If you only knew the half of it. All my floral orders came in a week late. The rush to get everything accomplished was the most enervating ordeal."

"No doubt," Tristan said, indifference coating his voice. "Mother, this is Alessia Weber. My date for the evening." One of his hands pressed into the small of my back and coaxed me forward. "Alessia, this is Evangeline Dufort, my mother."

She glanced at Tristan with a pointed look, slight irritation flaring, before quickly reigning her features back to doting host. "Alessia, what a pleasure to finally meet you." Her hand extended to me.

I accepted it. "Same, Mrs. Dufort." I smiled.

The man beside her finished with the conversation he was engaged in and directed his attention to me. "Evangeline, who is our lovely guest?" he asked.

"Tristan's date, darling. Alessia Weber." *Did I imagine the distaste when she said my name?*

"Well, so honored you could join us, Alessia. You look stunning, my dear." He took my hand and lightly kissed it, winking. *I see where Tristan learned his winsome ways.*

"You're seated at our table, Tristan. We must go, Lyle, and greet our other guests." Evangeline raised her elbow, indicating to her husband to take it.

"Something to drink?" Tristan said, which pulled my attention from the retreating couple.

"Would love one." I looked up at him and smiled. "A soda would be great."

"I'll be right back." He pulled out a chair for me from the table. I thanked him and sat.

Across from me, a girl approached the table and sat in one of the decorative chairs.

"I see Tristan's little infatuation continues," Opal said over the flute tipped toward her red lips. Lips to match her silky scarlet dress.

"I'm not sure what you mean." I had an idea what she may be referring to, but it seemed easier to play dumb than be spiteful.

She scoffed. "You're a smart girl, Alessia. A guy like Tristan has one woman leaving his arm as the next sinks into his other. This little hero bit he has going with you is cute, but it won't last. Trust me, I'm trying to do you a favor." She glimpsed behind me. "Or perhaps I'm too late." She smirked and took another drink.

Tristan sat down next to me, placing two glasses in front of us.

"Opal." He dipped his head in greeting. She tipped her glass to him in response and looked away.

I leaned into Tristan, whispering, "I take it she's not very excited to be here."

He sipped his drink, glancing at his sister. "Opal and I have attended many of our mother's events. And each holds the same wondering allure," he said with blatant sarcasm.

I nodded, catching on that the family dynamics were a tight ball of drama I didn't want to untangle.

The lights dimmed. Low rumbles of clapping filled the room, and Evangeline's voice projected through a microphone.

"Welcome, all of you! What another wonderful turnout for this year's benefit."

I twisted in my seat to gain a better view. She stood on a stage at the far end of the room. "This year's event is thanks to none other than the marvelous Vasili Incorporated and in honor of their valiant efforts through the Growth Foundation. As many of you know, the chief founder is none other than my dear husband, Lyle Dufort." She waved her hand. A light followed in that direction, illuminating a waving Lyle. "Along with the late Michael Vasili. Without their efforts, millions of children would lack the education they need. Due to the tragic loss of Michael, we wanted to take this year's event to recognize the valiant efforts of such an honorable man."

The stage went dark again, and a screen behind her lit up with pictures and music—a tribute video to the man she had mentioned.

"I need another drink." Opal got up and traipsed toward the drink bar.

"I don't think I ever connected that the Dufort's and Vasili's worked together," I mused aloud. "I've heard of Vasili. My dad's pretty invested in the technology/science world. Vasili Inc.: always on the cutting edge of technology."

"It is." Tristan sat relaxed in his chair, sipping his drink. "Yes, the Duforts joined forces with Vasilis nearly two decades ago. The sky has been the limit since. Although, it doesn't seem our sweet Opal would agree things are so rosy." He chuckled.

"And what would you say?"

He watched me as if measuring his next words. "I would say things aren't always what they appear on the surface."

Tristan's parents returned to the table, ending our conversation.

Opal also returned with another couple, whom Tristan introduced as his grandparents.

Servers arrived, offering the first course of the evening. A plate covered in fancy embellishments—that I didn't know if I was supposed to eat or not—and a filet of salmon over a bed of asparagus and lettuce greens sprinkled on top was sat in front of me.

Savory and delicious flavors burst in my mouth at first bite. Tantalizing my tastebuds and satisfying my stomach in wonderful ways. My dress was so fitted it tightened with each bite, making it hard to move.

Conversation around the table was very matter-of-fact, revolving mostly around the painstaking details of Evangeline's efforts in the evening's affairs.

"So what do your parents do, Alessia? Are you local or boarding with the school?" Lyle asked before placing another bite of food in his mouth.

"Oh, my father is a professor at Ridgecrest."

Evangeline pursed her lips.

"Ah, yes. Professor Weber. I do believe we have met a time or two," Lyle said.

"Really? I didn't realiz—"

"Lyle, I grow tired of your drivel. Isn't it bad enough that she is here?" Evangeline cut in with a harsh whisper. That was clearly heard by the whole table. She gave her son a severe look.

Tristan swiftly lifted his glass, swallowed his drink, and offered his hand to me."Care to dance?"

The sudden offer threw me, my thoughts still sifting through the comments at the table.

"Oh, sure." I placed my hand in his, the soft caress of his enveloped mine.

Other couples glided in sync with live instruments being played. We reached the center of the dance floor, Tristan moving my hand to his shoulder as he turned us to face each other. His hand rested along my back while the other gracefully slid across my arm, connecting our hands at the end.

"Do you know how to dance?" Green eyes connected with mine. Wanting. Desiring.

I swallowed. "A little."

Skill and precision moved us across the dance floor like floating on air. It seemed Tristan was very good at many things.

But this felt wrong.

Our movements flowed effortlessly across the floor. He twirled me and pulled me back against him.

Tristan was the safer option. He didn't bring about emotions that were too hard to deal with. His kindness and desire to protect me were admirable; they didn't stir anything more than that. I didn't feel a connection.

He dipped us, bringing our faces so close I thought he might kiss me. Our eyes interlocked again. My chest thumped with the unknown of the moment. I closed my eyes as he brought us out of the dip and swirled us smoothly into motion again. *No, this isn't right.*

It was wrong if he believed this was something more. No matter how hard I tried, my heart always belonged to someone else.

I needed to fix this.

"Tristan. I think we should talk. Somewhere private?"

A devious grin met my request. He nodded and, holding my hand, led us to the edge of the dance floor, to his family's table. Leaning in close to his father, he whispered something. Evangeline's eyes narrowed, looking up at Tristan.

"Be smart," she said to him before he returned to my side.

We left the bustle of the dining hall and into the much quieter hallway.

At the end of the hall was a set of dark wooden doors. Tristan opened them, revealing a large office space. He motioned for me to go first. The room was dark, light from the moon casting shadows through the window. Tristan walked over to the sofas and clicked on a lamp, chasing away the shadows and bringing the room's beauty to light. Built-in shelves covered three of the four walls, the fourth possessing a very large window.

"Is this private enough?"

I glanced around the room, rubbing my hands along my dress. "The hallway would have been fine, too. Whose office is this?" Moving a little further into the room, appreciating the layout and shelves of books, I reached the large arched window. Unable to focus on anything outside the window; my thoughts were too busy forming the right words I needed to say.

"My father's. A bit ostentatious if you ask me, but my father and I often don't see eye to eye." His voice drifted closer to me. Heat drifted against my back as his hands gently stroked my arms, sending shivers all over. My eyes squeezed shut, and I stepped forward out of his reach.

"I need to be honest with you. I'm so grateful for how you have helped me with everything. Seriously, I don't think I would be alive without you. But I also don't want to hurt you." I turned slightly, catching him in my peripheral. "I'm sorry, really I am, but I don't see the relationship going the same way I think you might."

He moved closer. "Tsk, tsk, tsk," his tongue clicked. Arms wrapped around me, pulling me tight against his chest. "Oh, sweet naive, Alessia. No worries, love," he whispered in my ear. "See, I used you too." *What?*

I moved to turn, but his grip tightened.

"What are you doing? Let me go!"

"You know, someone went through a lot of trouble to hide you, Butterfly. Quite the difficult catch, after all."

I squirmed against his hold, but he held fast.

"But even butterflies aren't impossible to capture. All that time, they were looking for a dead woman."—I stopped moving—"a daughter showing up threw a nice change in the game. The more pieces to play with the better, in my opinion. But I was supposed to eliminate the problem. The lure of the chase was far too appealing to pass, though. I had debated saving you for myself. Real shame it wouldn't have worked between us." He bent his head and nuzzled my neck. "Mmm, but how about we have a little fun first." He chuckled darkly. *What is he saying? What woman? He's supposed to eliminate the problem? This is bad. Really, really bad.*

Panic struck hard and fast. Frantically, I wriggled and squirmed. My arms were pinned, unable to maneuver my hands.

"Tristan, let me go! What are you even talking about?" I tried stomping on his foot, but he picked me up, moving us across the room.

Tears welled in my eyes, and a scream reached my lips, but his hand smothered it. His grip around me loosened from the slight hand adjustment, and I desperately clawed and scratched at the arm still holding me.

"Oww!" He bellowed and dropped me. I stumbled out of his reach, crawling as fast as I could. His hand grabbed my leg, slowly dragging me across the floor. "Not so fast, little Butterfly. I knew there was some fire in you."

I twisted and kicked with my free leg. He dodged it.

A loud crack flooded the room, and suddenly, the pressure holding my leg vanished.

"What the hell are you doing here? You were told your services were no longer needed." Tristan's anger laced every word.

"What I came here to do," another voice growled.

I knew that voice.

Beck? Why is Beck here?

Grunts and groans resounded before a loud thud hit the floor.

Moving again, I sat and scooted backward toward the sofa, panting. Sobs racked my body. Tears blurred my vision and streamed down my face.

Hurried steps hit the wood floor, drawing closer to me.

Two hands found my cheeks and brushed at the loose hair hanging around my face. I screamed and pulled away. "No! Please, don't."

The hands returned. Gentle and tentative.

"Shhh, Lissa. It's me. I'm not going to hurt you. Please." His voice cracked on the word *please.*

My hands covered his wrists, struggling to compose myself. So confused. Scared.

"I don't—I don't know what's happening," I sobbed, shaking my head. "I—I. He said someone wants me dead? And then he tried to—he tried to...." I shuttered.

"Alessia, listen to me. I'm here now. I know...." His head turned, cursing. "Can you walk? I need you to come with me."

"How? I don't know who to trust...." I whispered. "I can't."

"Lissa, it's me. You can trust me!" A fierceness imbued his voice.

Curls fell into my eyes as my head shook back and forth. Beck's hold strengthened, stopping my movements.

"I know things have been a real mess. I know you don't understand, but I will take you from here and get you somewhere safe. I can't protect you here anymore."

His determined eyes held mine. Tears still streamed down my face, his hold firm, waiting.

I wasn't sure what to do. Who to trust. But Beck had been an anchor in my life before, so I clung to that truth.

My decision must have shown on my face because Beck removed his hands and placed them in mine, pulling me to a stand. He released one hand, still holding the other, and we raced out of the office. Passing Tristan's unconscious body.

We fled through the hallway, out some side doors leading outside, running down a set of stairs.

Dashing through a wooded area, trees flashed by me, my dress catching and snaring on undergrowth. Roots, large and knotted, caused me to stumble. *Stupid heels.*

Beck paused as I righted myself, and we were running again. The treacherous ground turned into a smooth dirt path, and a small black car waited in the clearing. As I inspected the path closer, I realized it was some sort of road.

Beck released my hand and rushed to the driver's side.

"Get in!" His words, sharp and angry, caused me to hesitate. But I wasn't going back to that nightmare I had just experienced with Tristan, so I pushed forward. Not to mention, I had no idea where I was.

Before my door was even shut, Beck sped down the dirt road. I reached for my seat belt, fastening it. *I really hope I made the better choice here.*

Chapter 15

My elbow rested against the window as silent tears rolled down my cheek. Trees streaked by, intermittent with road signs. A large one for New York sticking out. That meant we were driving south. Blurry lights flickered through the windshield, and I swiped at the wet lines on my face while quietly examining the muddy splotches, rips, and tears on my gown.

I sat staring and realized I was finally in a position to talk to Beck. Sitting in a car right next to him, where he couldn't escape.

Not ready to dive too deep into all the questions swarming my thoughts, I went with the easy, most practical. "Where are we going?" My voice came out gravelly from lack of use.

His grip on the steering wheel loosened from the tight hold he had ever since we got in the car, but his attention remained on the road.

"New York."

I sighed. Obviously. That much I deduced on my own. "Why New York?"

He glanced briefly at me before his gaze returned to the road, his knuckles turning white on the steering wheel again.

"I can't take you back to the Academy. Not after what happened tonight." His words were clipped and enraged, and I involuntarily moved closer to the door, my arms wrapping around me.

"I'm sorry," he said with a deep sigh. "I'm not angry at you. Definitely not at you." His shoulders relaxed. "We're going somewhere safe. I didn't want it to go this way, but I wasn't realizing the threat level or how deep things went." His eyes peeked at me again. "There's a lot I need to tell you, but...we're not out of danger yet. Think you can follow my lead until we get there? Then I promise I will tell you what I know."

Tenderness in his words shattered what little composure I had managed, and tears started falling again. All I could manage was a nod.

I wanted to trust him, but there was also a lot I didn't know about Beck and his life. Maybe it was the connection we had, the one I thought we had lost long ago, or maybe I was acting like a naive and foolish girl again. Either way, this was the current path before me—only time would tell if I was right about him.

After two hours of driving, we reached the outer parts of the city. This area of town did not look friendly; it was the kind of area that called for locking your doors and praying you didn't get lost. We pulled into a self-storage lot, and Beck parked the car in front of one of the grey units.

"Is this where you hide my body?" I smirked, only half joking. Fighting off the real emotions that threatened to consume me. But this place *was* majorly creepy.

His head turned, and he side-eyed me, lips forming a flat line. I raised my eyebrows in question. He reached behind his seat and handed me a small drawstring bag. *Okay then. Not up for jokes.*

"Here. You can change out of that dress. We don't need it drawing attention at the airport."

"The airport?" I took the bag and stared at him. "Why are we going to the airport?"

He opened his door and got out. I watched him walk over to one of the garage-style doors at the end of the row and unlock it. He crouched and lifted the storage door open. Grabbing the door handle, I exited the car and joined him.

Inside the unit were stacks of labeled bins and an assortment of sports equipment, suitcases, various odds and ends of everyday useful things, and strange gear and equipment unfamiliar to me.

Beck moved in and started rifling through one of the bins, grabbing a java leather duffle bag. He threw some clothes and toiletries in it, along with what looked like a wallet with passports.

I examined the bag in my hands; opening it, I found a hoodie and a pair of jeans. I lifted the jeans, noting their size. They were my size.

"Why do you have clothes in my size?" I held the jeans out, questioning him.

"I called in a favor." He shoved a few more things in his bag and nodded to the pants in my hands. "We need to get going. I'll be in the car." He cleared his throat and walked out. *Man! His elusiveness was getting annoying.*

Confusion mixed with a high dose of curiosity kept me going. I quickly removed my dress, replacing it with the new clothes. Something needed done with my mess of hair, but I had nothing. A few finger combs would have to do.

I left the dress and hopped into the car. Beck watched me momentarily, then returned to the storage unit, closing and locking it.

We navigated through the city until we reached a parking service lot. Beck parked the car on the street outside the gates and dropped the keys in the cup holder. He leaned into the backseat to grab the duffel bag he had filled.

"Don't leave anything in the car." He stopped what he was doing and gave me a very serious look.

The clutch that held my phone and lipstick was left at the benefit on the table with Tristan's family. I had no money, no phone, no ID. *How am I going to fly somewhere? And where were we flying to?*

I raised my arms, showing empty hands.

Beck bounded out of the car. I followed. *Because what else am I to do? I agreed to this when he asked me to follow his lead. Did he have to make it so difficult, though?*

An airport shuttle bus sat at the entrance to the parking lot. We climbed aboard and sat in the first available seat. A sudden flashback of riding the bus to school together flitted through my mind as I watched the shuttle continue to fill. Soon, the driver shut the door and exited the gates, driving down the road.

My eyes moved to Beck. He was preoccupied with looking out the window. At first, he appeared indifferent, but I studied him further and noticed his leg bouncing and his hand flexing. *Was he nervous? What was he nervous about? Was he afraid someone was following us?*

My anticipation grew greater for answers. I didn't know what kind of answers Beck had. I did know he had them, though, and I had a feeling they went beyond what was happening tonight.

The shuttle arrived at the airport, and we hurried off.

Beck found the shortest line for check-in, and I stood next to his shoulder."I don't have any ID, Beck. I barely had anything on me at the benefit, and what I did have is still there." I said, giving him a pointed look.

"I have it taken care of." He approached the desk, handing the attendant two tickets and two passports. "Just a carry-on." He indicated the bag in his hand.

There was some typing on her computer, and she glanced a few times at us. What was he doing? Was he using a fake passport?

"Okay, you're all set," she stated. "Your flight number is here, and you'll find your terminal here." She circled some letters and numbers on the ticket.

"Thank you." Beck took the papers. He probably wouldn't have answered if I had asked, so I paid extra close attention as he slipped them into an outside pocket of the bag and caught a glimpse of the flight time on the ticket.

"Germany? We're going to Germany?"

Beck grabbed my hand. "Come on," he said.

Perhaps it was the heat from his hand or the fluttery movement happening inside me, but I thought I saw a small smile on Beck's face as we proceeded to security.

Beck

Holding her hand was probably a mistake. This whole plan was a mistake; this decision didn't affect just me, but I didn't know what else to do. I had to get her out. How she still trusted me, I had no idea. Since I arrived at Ridgecrest, my actions have been reckless and impulsive. Not focused. Not sure. I failed to know how to execute the next step. It made me feel out of control; I didn't do out of control. It was stupid to reveal myself to her; she didn't need to know I was there, but I couldn't stop myself. She was a force in my life I couldn't resist, but that complicated everything. We were on the run, and I didn't have a plan of what to do next.

They called our seat section, and we joined the line for boarding. Once on the plane and having her far away from all the threats, the rage that boiled right under the surface, ready to erupt and destroy everything around me, waned slightly. *She was safe.*

I've never wanted to hurt, even kill, someone more than I did upon entering that room she was in with Tristan. Luckily for him, her tears broke me, driving me to meet her needs and not break every bone in his body. And I needed to move her quickly; I only had a small window of time and wouldn't fail her again.

She sat beside me and fiddled with the strings on her hoodie, watching the people prep the plane from the window. It used to be so easy to talk to her. But casual conversation seemed inappropriate with everything that had happened between us. It made it hard to know where to begin.

My hand went to my head, brushing my hair back as I breathed deeply and exhaled through my mouth. I could still hear her sobs. In that room. His hands on her. I squeezed my eyes closed. I let it go too far. Removing her was the only way. *You're doing the right thing, Beck.*

Chapter 16

Eight hours on a plane next to Beck, and I still didn't have answers. Granted, I fell asleep for most of it. Drained from the traumatic upheaval in my life. I woke to drooling on Beck's shirt as the plane descended. "Sorry," I said, wiping it off with my sleeve. Heat rose to my cheeks. He shrugged like it was no big deal.

When we landed, Beck reached up to grab our only luggage from the overhead while we waited our turn for deboarding. Every time he moved, I felt it, even if he wasn't touching me. Like the flicker of a flame, and if I got too close, I'd burn.

There was so much I needed to talk to him about but didn't know where to start the conversation: Hey, I'm pretty sure you tried to kill me, but like an idiot, I followed you here, so let's talk. *That's not too bad, actually.*

After a quick pit stop at a car rental desk, we made our way to an indoor parking garage attached to the airport. The silence between us was getting intense. It pricked every time I looked at him or brushed against him. Beck must have felt it, too, because I was about to speak when we climbed into the car, but he beat me.

"Are you hungry? You slept through the meal on the plane."

Food was a good place to start, I guess.

"I could eat," I said.

We drove about five minutes from the airport and stopped at a fast-food burger place. Beck parked, reached into his leather bag, and handed me some money.

"Get whatever you'd like," he said.

"You're not coming in? Don't you want anything?" I was a little nervous. I'd never been to a foreign country before. But food was food, right? It couldn't be that hard.

Beck shook his head. "Nah, I'm good."

I entered the restaurant and found the ordering counter. The menu was all in German. *Great, I don't know German.*

The only words I understood were burger, bacon, and BBQ. I chose the option with those three things and hoped for the best. The cashier was friendly, but he also only spoke German. *What was my life right now?*

Ten minutes later, I was climbing back into the car with a bag of food. My mouth salivating. It smelled so good. A loud growl rumbled in my belly, and Beck peeked at me with raised eyebrows. I scrunched my nose. "Guess I didn't realize how hungry I was."

Beck's head fell against the headrest while he tapped a small black phone on his leg.

I set my bag in between us. "Have some fries," I offered with a tiny smile, digging into my burger. He covertly eyed the bag, and one side of his lip lifted.

While I folded the wrapper around my burger, I watched his hand snag a couple of fries. Taking a bite, a smile grew around my food.

"What's this?" He waved a napkin at me.

Pressing my fingers to my mouth, I swallowed. "Looks like a napkin, Beck."

He stopped waving it and held it open, raising an eyebrow. Several numbers were scrolled across it. *Maybe a phone number.*

I shrugged my shoulders.

"Was your cashier male?" he asked.

"Yeah."

A low chuckle left him.

"Of course," he muttered.

The phone he was fiddling with rang. Beck picked it up and cursed. He squeezed the bridge of his nose and answered the call.

"Did you make it out?" I heard an unclear voice come through the phone next to Beck's ear. Whoever it was was practically shouting.

"I said not to call me till later," he said, annoyance clear in his voice. "Yeah, we're out."

"Good. It didn't take them long to get on me. Tristan was all over me about infringement. He's claiming a kidnapping and wants her back alive. I don't know why, but they want your girl bad. And now they want you dead. There's big money behind this. I bailed right after I finished your favor. You cost me a lot on this one, Cirillo. Consider my debt paid in full. Watch your back." And then they ended the call.

Beck tossed the phone in the center console before running his hands down his face. Meanwhile, I sat facing him, scowling. He noticed and reached for the ignition. I leaned forward and grabbed his hand.

"Seriously?" I snapped. "No more, Beck. I've been patient. But what the heck? Who was that calling? Talking about kidnapping and people wanting me. And you dead for helping me? Tell me what you know," I pleaded, unable to keep the tears from filling my eyes.

He stared at our hands momentarily before bringing his eyes in line with mine. Eyes that always pulled me in, making me feel safe and wanted.

"Trust me, it's a lot. And I'm gonna tell you everything. I'm sorry. I tried so hard to keep you out of it."

"Keep me out of it? I'm in it," I fumed, pulling back from him.

"You're right. Since we have a bit of a drive, I guess the best place to start is with my family." He started the car and backed out of the parking lot.

"Around two hundred years ago, 10 families formed a guild known as the Verndari Order, which means to protect. The Verndari was established as an international guard, a set of highly trained individuals who would act in service of protection. An elite force to be used for guarding against or eliminating threats."

I was unsure where he was going with this. "Like the CIA?"

"Not quite. A Verndari's scope is broader and through private contracting. No government regulates them, but rather through a council within the organization."

"What does this have to do with your family?"

"My family? We are members of the Verndari and have been as far back as the beginning of the guild. It's very old. They work in secrecy and strive to keep it heavily guarded. That's why I never told yo —"

A laugh burst from my lips. "I'm sorry, what?"

His eyes glanced at me, confusion marring his face.

"Beck, come on. You're serious?"

"Why would I make something like this up?" His focus returned to the road.

"Wait, you're serious, aren't you?

"Maybe you should have paid closer attention when your history professor was teaching on secret societies," he said.

I gaped at him and then cleared my throat. "Sorry, it was a little much. Continue."

"When I was little and lived in your neighborhood, my parents had gone dark in the organization, wanting to raise a family. But they also knew there was a training facility not far away when the time came. Mom and Dad wanted their children to receive the best training before returning to international fieldwork. At age 13, I began my Verndari training. And three years later, when you moved away,"—he shook his head and exhaled— "I didn't know how to keep lying to you. I was tired of keeping secrets. So I pulled away; I wasn't allowed to tell you anything. My parents warned me to keep my distance from you. Your leaving seemed like a sign I was making the right choice."

"That's why you never reached out after I left," I murmured.

He glanced at me with that sad look he always gave me. "It was the way it was meant to be. It was better for you not to be involved in my life."

I looked away and straightened, swiping my hand through my hair. "So say I believe you and this secret spy agent story. Why tell me now? What does all this have to do with me? Why were you at Ridgecrest? Why were you involved in trying to murder me?" *And why did you ignore me?* I kept that to myself; I wouldn't let Beck know how much I cared.

He flicked on the turn signal and took the next exit.

"The woman you know as Chelsea? That was her on the phone. Her name isn't Chelsea; that's her alias. She is also part of the Verndari. She received an anonymous contract for a hit on you about two months ago. The contract was to be handled as life-threatening, meaning they wanted the threat taken out. You were the threat. She dropped your name while at the German training grounds a few days before she planned to leave. I knew something was off with the negotiations. Why would you be a threat to anyone?"

"Someone set up a contract to have me killed?" I whispered. My head turned away, glancing out the window, thoughts whirling. "Who? Why?" I asked, snapping my attention back to him.

His head shook. "We don't know. I didn't even know Tristan was involved until the night of the benefit.

I followed Chelsea to sabotage her attempts. I was there to eliminate the threat against your life and figure out what was going on."

Beck was right. All this was a lot. He was like a secret agent. All this time, he had this hidden life, living in secret. And someone was trying to kill me. *I think I need to sit down. I was sitting down. I need some air.*

I pressed the button to put down the window, letting the cool air whip against my face. I was still deciding what to ask next. There was so much more to uncover, but I needed a moment.

All of this sounded so crazy, but in some weird way, it fit. How else would he get into Ridgecrest? How would he get me out of the country so easily? He had fake passports. I wanted it to be true because that would mean he wasn't trying to murder me but to protect me. But it still meant someone was trying to kill me.

I looked away from the window, my eyes studying him. "What about all the times you were the guilty one? They caught you on the cameras that night of the attack in the locker rooms. The night I was poisoned, you gave me a drink. I've struggled to believe you would do anything like that, but,"—I returned to watching out the window—"it's clear I don't know you like I thought...." I trailed off, mulling over all that he'd shared so far.

He reached over, grabbing my hand.

"I know. I know there is a lot I need to explain, but if you're willing to hear me out, I'm ready to tell you." He squeezed my hand and furrowed his brows. "But first, my family," he sighed deeply.

He released my hand and turned us down a long driveway. Tall pines lined the drive and circled around a beautiful two-story house of gray and black tones, a combination of stone walls and floor-to-ceiling windows. A home fitting for the hills of ski country.

Two teen boys were wrestling on the ground in the front yard as we pulled up to the house, our arrival pulling their attention.

We climbed out of the car, and they scurried over to us.

"Beck! You're back," the taller one exclaimed as he approached. He was almost as tall as Beck. His dark hair was longer at the top and more full towards the front. His brown eyes reminded me so much of Beck's. I knew this boy.

"Ben?" I asked in disbelief. Beck's younger brother smiled at me.

"That's right. Not the puny little squirt you remember, right?" He came up to me, giving me a big bear hug. Easily lifting me off the ground.

"Hey, Alessia," the other boy said and also approached me with a hug but was more gentle in his method.

"Conrad? Wow, you've grown," I said, hugging him back.

"Man, it's good to see you," Ben said with another big smile.

Warm sensations of happiness flourished inside me at his words. Seeing Beck's brothers took me back to a simpler time, a time when I wasn't entangled in secrets and lies.

"Beckett," a stern voice came from the upper balcony of the house. Our heads moved to face that direction. Beck's mom stood there, her face solemn, and her long black hair floated slightly against the wind.

"We need to get inside," Beck said. He grabbed the leather bag and, with a lift of his chin, suggested I follow him.

Slapping and laughter passed me as Ben and Conrad darted through the main entrance to the house. Beck shook his head, extending his arm for me to go first.

Inside was a large kitchen and living space, the windows brightening the room with sunlight. Thalia Cirillo walked down the stairs, and a well-formed man dressed in a suit stood at the kitchen island—Marcus Cirillo. He was reading something on his phone before he peered up at the commotion coming into the home.

"Hello, Alessia," Thalia greeted me with a friendly smile. She then fixed a displeased glare on her son. "I wish our reunion was on better terms." Her pointer and middle fingers pressed at her temples as if pained. "What were you thinking, Beck?"

"Mom, you can't be serious?" Beck disputed, disbelief charging his words. He stood staring at her with his arms wide. An unhumorous laugh left him. "They were going to kill her! You just wanted me to let that happen?"

"I wasn't given a chance to form an opinion when I'm just learning of it 20 minutes before her arrival," Thalia said.

Beck's dad, Marcus, joined us by the entrance. "Maybe this is a conversation for a more private setting?" he interposed with a pointed look in my direction.

Thalia nodded in agreement. "She can use your room, and you'll stay in Ben's. Once she is settled, meet your father and me in the dining room." Her words were directed to Beck. "It really is good to see you, Alessia." She turned and went to the kitchen.

Beck tossed his bag over his shoulder, walking to the stairs with me trailing behind him. *How was I even to begin making sense of all this?*

Chapter 17

At the top of the stairs was an open loft with bookshelves and furniture and a hallway leading to more rooms. We walked to the first door on the right. Beck opened it and showed me into his room. A simple space decorated in greens and blues greeted me with a bed, a dresser, and a desk. Wide windows overlooking a wooded area.

"This is it. The bathroom is down the hall, second door on the left. Anything you might need, just let me know."

"I think I'm good right now. Thank you." I surveyed the room; it smelled of citrus and balsam and something that drew me back to childhood laughter. I smiled as childhood memories of playing with Beck sprang to mind. *Am I really in Beck's bedroom? In Germany!*

Movement caught in my peripheral as Beck turned to leave through the door.

"Beck?" I blurted.

He paused in the hallway, hand on the door frame, his face engaged, ready to listen. So many unanswered questions, so much I didn't understand, but I was grateful. And he clearly was in some kind of trouble with his parents. "Thank you."

He smiled and withdrew from the room.

Moving over to the bed, I sat and bent over, my face in my hands. I released a long breath. And then I was on my feet again, pacing, running my hands through my hair. Everything was happening so fast. Someone was trying to murder me. Beck and his whole family had a hidden life. I needed a plan. A plan would help things feel more stable and give me direction. First, I would give Beck his time with his parents, and then he and I would have a serious talk. *Yeah, see, I can do this.*

Footsteps hurried past the room but stopped and returned to the doorway. A head popped in. Ben pressed his finger to his lips and waved me to follow with his other hand.

We crept down the hall, back to the loft at the top of the staircase. Below, we could hear disgruntled voices speaking.

Ben signaled me to be quiet again before squatting behind the half wall next to the staircase. I sat beside him and focused more intently on the conversation happening below. A smidge of guilt went through me for eavesdropping, but the secrets were piling up, and I wasn't sure I could trust anyone to give me the truth.

"She knows," Beck admitted with some irritation.

"What does she know? How much have you told her?" Thaila asked.

Beck sighed. "She knows who we are, what we do, and how I found her. I can't lie to her, not anymore. She was scared and needed to know so she could trust me."

Marcus cleared his throat. "This could put her in more danger than she already is. The Verndari keep their matters guarded."

Tension between the three talking downstairs could be felt from where I was sitting. Clearly, Mr. And Mrs. Cirillo were unaware of what Beck had been doing for the past month in the States.

"This will have consequences, Beckett, not just for you, but for her. You don't even know who assigned the contract.

Why didn't you tell us?" Thalia's voice was passionate, filled with emotions. Grief. Fear. Anger.

"You don't think I know the danger she's in? I've spent the last month digging to find who's behind all this so I could figure out how to get her out. I didn't plan to bring her here." Beck said, fervor creeping into his words. "I didn't see another way. And once I compromised my position, I had to tell her."

There was a momentary silence.

"So what's your plan?" Marcus said, calm and low.

"Other than hiding her until I figure out a way to ensure she's safe, I'm still working on it," Beck mumbled.

"What else do we need to know?" Thalia asked reluctantly.

"They've put a new hit out that includes me."

"This isn't like you, Beck. This is sloppy work. You're too close to this, and you got noticed. What alias did you use? We need to get on damage control," Marcus said, the calmness gone from his voice.

Beck hesitated. "I used my first name but changed the last."

Marcus's ire continued to increase. "I presume you have a good reason for that?" he growled.

"She was there, Dad. She would have known. It was riskier not to use my name and have her blow my cover." There was a sound of defeat in Beck's words.

"Oh, Beck," Thalia sympathized.

"This was foolish," Marcus hissed. "There were better ways."

Beck's tone hardened. "What's done is done. Don't put this through the Order. It stays within our family. Ben can handle the cover up."

Ben moved a bit beside me and hugged my knee. A question in his eyes. I shrugged my shoulders. I was of no help to him. I still needed so many things cleared up myself.

Beck wasn't supposed to come to Ridgecrest.

But he did.

For me.

"I can tell you are upset; I understand that. I don't wish harm to Alessia, Beck. But you should have involved us. Gone in with a better plan," Marcus said.

Silence.

"Talk with Ben. See what he can uncover. And he needs to make your abysmal attempt at an alias disappear," Marcus concluded the conversation, and I heard the scrape of chairs on the floor.

Ben grabbed my hand with lightning speed and pulled me down the hallway just as footsteps could be heard coming up the stairs.

He pushed me back into Beck's room. *Stay cool*, he mouthed. I stared at him, dumbfounded, and it wasn't long before Beck appeared in the doorway.

"Oh, hey, Beck-aroo. I was just making sure Alessia was doing okay." Ben grinned.

Beck gave a skeptical look but didn't press the matter. "I need you to do a database run on Tristan Dufort. He's the only lead I have right now. Find out everything you can. I want names on all associates, family history and records, criminal background, underhand dealings, the works, Ben."

Ben's forehead wrinkled, and he scrunched his nose. "That's gonna take some time. I'll see what I can do. But, uh, shouldn't we work on making you two disappear first? That sounds like more fun anyway." Ben slapped his hands and rubbed them together.

Beck ran a hand down his face. "Right. I know—wait a minute." Curious brown eyes tossed between Ben and me. "You two were listening, weren't you? And Mom and Dad think they have their hands full with me." His smirk turned to a smile, and a small chuckle left him.

"Well, guess I better get to work." Ben smiled and tapped his brother on the shoulder before exiting the room.

Beck's gaze drifted to me, and a soul-stirring smile slammed into me, knocking my heart rate up a few notches, but his eyes held uncertainty.

One foot stepped closer to me. "I have a place I'd like to show you. If you're not too tired."

I wanted so badly to fall back into an easy rhythm with him. The way it used to be. But what if that was all a lie, too. *What if I can't trust him?*

My delay must have caused him to second guess. He started to back up. "Maybe some time to rest? I imagine you feel tired from...." He trailed off, and his eyes diverted to the window.

"No, I want to know what's going on. And right now, you're about my only option. I don't even have my phone or a way to leave..." My hand went to my head. "Ava! The school! She has to be worried sick. I've been staying with her. What if Tristan tries to hurt her? What if he tells her you did something to me? And the school. What—what are they going to think?"

Beck's smile vanished, and in its place, a deep frown, his brows creased with regret. "I'm sorry, Alessia. You can't contact Ava or the school. We'll have to let some things play out until we plan the next step."

"What—what if they call my dad? You're not going to let me call my dad? Am I a prisoner here now? Your parents don't even want me here!" Tears started to well up, and my breathing turned shallow. I didn't want to cry, but it was all too much. The storm of emotions inside me was getting harder to ignore.

Strong, secure arms wrapped around me, pulling me into a tender embrace.

"Hey," he said softly, "I know what that might have sounded like. My parents aren't blaming you. If I had gone to them before, they would have helped me protect you. I screwed up. I didn't think. My only focus was I had to get to you as soon as possible." He stroked a hand down through my hair. "You're not a prisoner, but this is where you are safest right now. I promise we won't forget about your dad. Right now, we are hiding, though." He pulled back and lifted my chin.

"Tell me what happened at Ridgecrest," I whispered.

His stare never left mine. He grasped my hand. "Walk with me?"

We left the house through the back door and entered the thick woods just beyond the small backyard. Branches cracked under my feet, and a chipmunk darted past as if spooked by the noise. The woods were almost magical, full of wonder and adventure, like walking into a faerie fantasy book. Beck led me deeper, the trees thinning until the greenery separated into an opening next to a flowing stream.

The tranquil babble of the water flowing over the rocks, and birds chirping and fluttering about instantly filled me with peace and quiet. It made sense why Beck would like this spot. He always enjoyed the outdoors.

We sat down next to the stream, watching the woods come alive. Leaves rustled from critters scurrying about. Insects buzzed. The plunk of a pebble hit the water as Beck tossed it.

I didn't want to disturb such a peaceful moment, but...

"Can I trust you?" I asked.

Another splash from his stones responded.

He turned to look at me. "You can trust me, Lissa," he said in earnest.

A small, humorless laugh escaped me. "Why keep me in all the lies and secrets at school? What really happened?"

"Chelsea was instructed to make your death look like an accident, and it needed to be done before your dad landed in Japan. She lured you to the coffee shop using Ava and planned to dismantle your brakes. I was outside the coffee shop. You saw me on the crotch rocket. She knew I would stop her. "

"Wait, really? Wow. And the wreck on the highway?"

"Coincidence. But turned out Chelsea's plan worked in our favor." Beck tossed a few more stones with more force than before.

"Chelsea still wasn't ready to work with me. She stuck close with Ava to determine where you would be and create an opportunity. The library's fire suppression system was an easy avenue. I tried to get you out before she released the alarm. But she found me and argued with me. I barely found you in time."

"It was you?" My hand moved to my parted lips. "Why did you leave? Why didn't you say something?"

"Revealing myself would have been more dangerous. Tristan and Andrew were already taking notice by that point. I didn't know their involvement at the time, but now it makes sense why they were watching me so closely. And then —" He paused, grabbing a few more rocks from around him, squeezing them tight in his fist.

"Andrew followed you into the locker rooms the night you were attacked. I never left after I bumped into you earlier that night—I stayed. Watching." He shook his head and stood, dropping the rocks. "I rushed in behind him, pushing him away from you, and we got into it. I knocked him out and took you home. I was so relieved when I saw you still breathing."

"You saved me. Twice. I couldn't remember anything after being knocked out." I pulled my knees up, resting my chin on them. It was him every time. But what about the yacht party. The poison.

He glanced over at me. "I stayed that time. And I would have stayed all night if Ava hadn't shown up."

"Tristan sent Ava. He told her to check on me," I said.

"He was using others to keep his hands clean. He wasn't going to dirty his own. And...I saw the shift happen right in front of me. My gut wasn't wrong about him. I should have listened to it." He kicked the ground and started pacing.

"What do you mean?"

"He started to get sweeter, right? More thoughtful, bring you flowers." He scoffed. "But I never wanted to involve you."

"Which was stupid, by the way," I said.

" I was going to get in and out once you were safe. I had to change tactics, though. He was suspicious and always around you."

"And the yacht?" This was the hardest one. I couldn't figure out how Beck wasn't at fault. *Please let me be wrong.*

Beck winced, and his face morphed as if tasting something bitter. "I finally convinced Chelsea to allow me to be the one to take you out. I would make it look like you died, and we would disappear. Chelsea would still fulfill her contract, and you would be out of harm's way. I planned to make you sick; you would then go home, and I would set the scene. Convincing everyone you were dead. I was going to tell you everything that night."

He didn't just say that!

I stood and crossed my arms, anger brewing like a bad storm. "You poisoned me? It *was* you?"

His shoulders shifted inward, and wrinkles formed as his face furrowed. "It wasn't like that. I didn't give you enough that it would hurt you, just enough to make you sick."

I shoved his shoulder, barely moving him, and narrowed my eyes. "How does that make it better?"

"Look, I had to get you out but not make it obvious what I was doing. Causing you to leave the party, making it look like I poisoned you, was a smart tactic."

I moved closer and shoved him harder; he stumbled back. "Beck, I couldn't walk! The doctor said I could have died if I had more of whatever you gave me."

Beck rolled his eyes, indignant. "But I knew how much I gave you. You were fine! Yes, it would make you sick, which was why I was with you when I gave it to you," he challenged.

"Maybe you don't recall leaving me to play in the pool with Charlotte." *Apparently still salty about that one.*

He sighed and took a step closer, his frustration palpable. "I didn't plan on walking away. Dancing with you. Being so close to you. You have any idea how crazy unfocused you make me?"

He moved another step closer fully into my space. His warmth. His smell. It all surrounded me.

"Watching you struggle because of my choice was the last thing I wanted to do, but I needed you out of danger. I walked away to clear my head; that was it. You were supposed to keep dancing, and I would have helped you off the boat when you felt the effects. But I messed up." His hand cupped my cheek, effectively weakening my outrage.

"I'm sorry, Lissa. You deserved better. I never wanted you to get hurt. I only wanted to protect you."

His words were sweet, and even though at the moment I didn't want it to, his touch made me feel all fluttery inside.

But it wasn't that easy. He'd lied. And had been lying. I wanted to trust him, but how did I know if I could? *He literally just admitted to nearly killing me!*

I pulled away from him and turned toward the way we came. "I want to go back now."

Chapter 18

"Three kings. Don't make me hurt you, Conrad," Ben said, placing his card on the center pile.

He watched as his brother snagged a quick bite of pizza from across the dining room table.

"Bullshit," Conrad called, narrowed his eyes at Ben, and waited.

Ben slapped the cards on the table and glared at him. He then pulled the large pile of cards from the center into his hand and added them to his other cards.

"You made it so obvious you were lying. You need to be quicker. Try more confidence in your words," Conrad said.

"How about I try shoving that pizza down your throat. Stop slowing everything down. Just play the game," Ben countered.

Beck chuckled as Conrad laid down two cards, calling two aces. Followed by Beck's one 2 and my one 3.

Beck leaned close to my shoulder, and the tingly sensation his presence so often brought blared to life.

"I'm pretty positive that was a lie," he whispered.

I didn't look at him, but I felt the intensity of his gaze regardless.

"Well, you'd be pretty used to those, wouldn't you." It was a low blow, and I instantly felt bad when Beck frowned and pulled back. I hadn't talked to him since the woods earlier, hiding out in his room until he told me there was pizza downstairs to eat.

Ben and Conrad called out their cards.

"Two 6s." Beck laid the cards down, still staring at me. A challenge.

I watched him, searching for any deceit. Beck always struggled to lie to me. It was never in his posture, always in the eyes. They held a sadness in them. Like it hurt him to keep anything but the truth from me.

"Bullshit," I said, smirking.

He kept eye contact as he picked the cards up from the center and placed them in his hand.

Those tingles began to warm, and I suddenly wanted to be a whole lot closer to him.

"You sure I'm the one you want to share a room with tonight, Beck?" Ben snickered, and Conrad joined him.

Beck sat up straighter and glared at Ben. I looked away and fiddled with my cards.

"One 7," I said, laying my card down, and play continued.

Beck challenged me to spot his lie, and I did. He was proving his integrity. That I know him. This caused a severe emotional crisis within me. Battling with the betrayal of his secrets, yet longing to be near him, to feel his hand in my hand, to laugh and joke with him. Is *he still the same old Beck I grew up with?*

"Alessia, do you want to see my rock collection?" a sweet young voice said from the left of me.

Beck's youngest brother, Jasper, with the biggest brown eyes I'd ever seen, stood beside me with two bags, one in each hand.

"Oh," I was going to say I would love to, but a loud male voice interrupted as a tall, dark-haired guy walked in from the main door.

"Hey-O, my people! What's this? Starting the party without me?" He looked to be around my age, maybe a little older. He moved through the kitchen, flipping the lid of one of the pizza boxes and letting it fall. "Beck, you don't even tell me you're back. I gotta hear it from this guy here?" he said, waving his hand toward Ben.

Beck smiled and stood up to greet the boy. He grabbed his hand, pulling him close, and both slapped a hand on the back.

"And who is this? A much more pleasant sight than you three jokers." The newcomer winked at me.

"Sorry, my return was a little crazier than planned," Beck said.

"I can see that," he said with a grin, a mischievous glint in his eyes, as he offered me his hand. "Ryder."

"Alessia." I took his hand and gave it a firm squeeze.

"I think I like you." He smiled and released my hand.

Clapping his hands together, he moved and sat in the chair behind Jasper.

"Deal me in, boys. What are we playing?"

"Actually, now that you're here, we should work out that thing I mentioned to you." Ben shoved the last of his crust into his mouth.

"It's always work with you guys, isn't it? Alright." Ryder shook his head and stood back up.

"I needed some fresh eyes. And your knack for sniffing out the finer details most of us miss," Ben said, standing with him.

"I'm already here, man. You can tone down the sweet talk," Ryder said.

They continued their chattering and headed toward a set of stairs led downstairs.

Beck moved to get up, tapping my arm.

"Hey! What about our game?" Conrad cried, dropping his cards in front of him.

"Later," Beck yelled over his shoulder.

I followed him to the same stairs Ben and Ryder went down.

At the bottom of the stairs was a carpeted room with couches, TVs, and video games, even a pool table. On the far left wall were two dark wooden doors. One led to what looked to be a bathroom and the other an office space. They went through the office door, and Beck and I followed.

Four large computer screens hung on the right wall, creating a large square. Under them was a long desk with an elaborate keyboard and control panel. High-back office chairs with wheels sat in the middle of the room.

Ryder turned, noticing Beck and me following, his eyebrows slightly furrowed. "Did I miss something?" He pointed at me.

"She's the whole reason I'm working on finding intel," Ben said.

Beck didn't respond, his attention on the screens.

"Guess there's a lot we need to catch up on," Ryder said, nodding at Beck.

Ben sat and swiveled the chair, typing some things into the computer. "I asked Ryder for help because I've hit a roadblock. This Tristan guy is clean in every area I've checked. He has questionable friends with some history but mostly money laundering and drugs. The family name has strong connections to some big tech companies and even is partners with Vasili Inc. There could be potential they would know about the Order, but other than that, I'm not finding much," he said

"I'm going to need a little more help here. Why are you digging into this guy?" Ryder asked.

"He tried to kill Alessia," Ben said like it was no big deal, but it freaked me out every time I heard it said out loud.

Ryder's head whipped in my direction.

"This is your 'in and out' case you took on in the States?" His gaze examined me, but his question was directed at Beck.

I squirmed a little under his scrutiny.

Beck finished reading something on one of the screens and turned toward Ryder.

"Alessia's an old family friend. She needed help with a life-threatening situation. It got complicated." He frowned.

"That's an understatement," Ben mumbled. Beck swatted the side of Ben's head.

"This little punk contracted a hit through the Verndari?" Ryder asked, squinting at a picture of Tristan on the screen.

"We don't know who did. It was anonymous. My instincts tell me Tristan is a pawn in the game. Someone else is pulling the strings. Tristan is arrogant and is used to being the one in charge. Which means it will be someone he is either in debt to or is close with," Beck said.

"How do we figure out who that is, and why would they be after me?" I voiced.

"It's exactly those pieces that will help us figure it out. This family has money, lots of it. My bet is all this relates to money. Greedy buggers are always thinking about it," Ryder said.

"Pull up what you have on the Dufort family, Ben," Beck said. "You think the family knew? He wasn't being swayed by an outside source? I didn't consider that. Where's the connection to Alessia?" Beck asked more to himself.

"I didn't say that, but the family would be worth looking into," Ryder said.

Ben grinned. "I like where you guys are going with this. Check this out. I found a trail of bleeding funds. Several off-the-books investments are in the red and attached to the

Dufort name. But I just uncovered them; they're buried under this nonprofit—The Growth Foundation."

I knew that name. Where did I hear that name before?

"He's hiding accrued debt on failed investments so that future investors only see profits," Ryder suggested.

"Most likely," Ben agreed.

"What does any of that have to do with me? My family doesn't have money." I asked.

Beck had been leaning against the desk, pensive and quiet. "Maybe it doesn't have to do with you having money but knowing secrets," he said. "People, especially those with a great deal to lose, will do anything to keep it. Ben, do you have a list of the big tech companies Dufort is associated with?"

Ben hit a few keys on the keyboard.

"Alessia, do you know the company hosting your dad's trip?" Beck looked at me.

"No, some research facility in Japan. But the school sent him."

"Let's see, Lyle Dufort has ties with three energy companies and an Institute of Technology in Japan." Ben leaned back in his chair, looking smug.

"How connected is Dufort to Ridgecrest, besides his son going there," Beck requested.

Ben didn't miss a beat. "Highly. He's on the school board and a big contributor."

"The school's in his pocket, then. I'm tracking you, Beck," Ryder said.

"I'm not. Can someone please explain," I said.

Beck stopped pacing and ran his hand through his hair. "When was the last time you talked with your dad?"

"Several days ago...but what does this have to do with my dad?"

"Does your dad own any stocks, or would he be involved in investment deals?" Ryder inquired, following Beck's line of thinking.

I shook my head. Dad never talked to me about anything other than his work. If he did any investing, I wouldn't know about it.

"Look up..." Beck began.

"Already on it." Ben's fingers flew across the keyboard. "It looks like Mr. Weber has a few shares in some high-end tech companies and a simple 401k. None of this looks connected with Dufort, though." Ben shook his head. "I'll keep digging. Maybe he's connected with one of the bleeding investments."

Beck nodded. "Let me know as soon as you have something."

Ben saluted and went back to the computer.

"If Tristan's family is behind initiating the contract on your life, it's possible all this is connected to the bleeding funds. The piece of sending your dad away has me thinking he's connected as well. We'll need to keep uncovering details, but it could be your dad is part of these off-the-book accounts and knows too much information. And anyone with too much information about these accounts has the potential to be damaging to Dufort," Beck said.

"If he's threatening to go public, why not just take out the Dad?" Ryder asked.

"Maybe she's a warning. I'll have to look more into her dad and his connection. I'm guessing he holds more value to them somehow," Beck replied.

Beck pressed his hand into my back and led us out of the room. I shivered. *Oh, these darn tingles.*

"I'll catch up with ya later, Beck," Ryder hollered.

We climbed the stairs, and I covered a yawn with my hand.

"It's been a long, long day. Why don't you head up to bed, and we can talk more about all this tomorrow," Beck said, rubbing a hand up my back.

"Yeah, that's probably a good idea."

Beck stayed downstairs, helping his younger brother Conrad clean up all the pizza boxes while I grabbed a quick shower and changed into a big t-shirt Beck had left me on his bed. When I finally crawled into bed, the soft comfort enveloped me, along with the smell of Beck. Balsam and citrus. It was everywhere. And it smelled amazing. *This boy, I can't keep him out of my head?*

Sheets bunched under me from tossing back and forth so much. All that had happened in the last 24 hours kept my brain from shutting off. My body longed for the rest. Another hour passed. A long sigh left me.

Shadows moved by the door, and I quickly sat up.

The figure moved a finger to their lips. "Shh, it's just me," Beck whispered. "The stars are amazing tonight."

Walking over to a window on the opposite wall, he opened it and glanced back at me. "You comin'?"

I crawled out of bed and slinked over to look out the window. It opened to a sloped roof over the back porch. Beck lifted one leg, placed it outside the window, and stepped onto the roof. The other leg slid smoothly out after.

The next moment, his hand appeared in front of me. A giddiness ran all the way to my toes. Reaching out, I closed my hand around his. It was firm. Safe. Right.

I pushed up with my foot as he pulled, slipping through the window.

On the roof, my eyes adjusted, and the scenery around me awakened. Massive trees around the property were dark splotches highlighted by the faint glow of twinkling stars and the glow of moonlight. A light breeze moved and rustled them. While an owl hooted in the distance.

My arm bumped into him when we sat down next to each other. Because we were close. So close I felt the heat from his body seeping into my side. And without a conscious decision of my own, I leaned even closer.

I gazed at the stars, grateful the silence between us wasn't awkward. The moment was merging past and present. Making everything in between insignificant, and only minutes had passed between us, not years.

"Do you remember that time we tried staying up all night to count the stars?" Beck chuckled.

I couldn't help the smile that spread across my face. I nudged his leg with my elbow.

"Yeah, and the number of Red Bulls we consumed to try to make it happen," I said

He shook his head, the smile slowly fading from his face.

"I'm sorry I didn't explain better when I got to the school. I was...I was afraid if I let you get close to me, I wouldn't be able to let you go." His head bowed, and he ran his fingers along the shingles. "And clearly, I was right," he mumbled.

Returning my gaze to the stars, I flipped my palm face up and extended it between us. He grabbed it, squeezed, and pulled it close to him, his thumb rubbing circles along my knuckles and across the back.

"Do you really think this is all because my dad is connected with some money scandal?"

"It's a high probability. And our only lead at the moment. I'll bring Mom and Dad up to speed. Get their thoughts. They've been doing stuff like this far longer than me."

"All that time they were looking for a dead woman." Words from Tristan came back to me from the night of the benefit.

"But Tristan mentioned they were looking for my mom," I said.

Beck's head tilted, thinking. "Then perhaps your dad has been mixed up with Dufort longer than we realize."

"Do you think that's how he got the job at Ridgecrest in the first place?"

"Maybe," he said thoughtfully.

"And what if because they can't find me, they go after my dad?"

"Ben's a master with hacking into places he doesn't belong. I'll have him locate your dad, and we can check in on him. Okay?"

Beck was so calm about all this. I didn't know how he did it. I wanted all the answers right now and for life to return to normal. *If only it were that easy.*

My mind was tired, and the rhythmic circles on my hand lulled me into tranquility. Or was it the boy I was sitting next to. The peace he brought confirmed what I always knew but never wanted to admit. No matter how terrifying it would be to care so deeply, to let Beck in, he already was. I trusted him. Needed his silent support. The solid rock he always was when my life crumbled around me. And I was starting to think that might be okay.

Chapter 19

"**B**eck, why did you climb so high? You know I can't climb that high." I looked up at the top of the oak tree, which sat at the edge of the woods, down at the end of our street. Where nine year old Beck sat laughing.

"All you have to do is face your fears, Lissa. You know you can trust me." Beck continued chuckling. He thought he was so clever by always outdoing me. He was competitive like that. He made everything a game where he became the hero because I would get scared. Well, not this time.

"Okay, I'm gonna do it." I grabbed the branch closest to the ground and placed my foot on the trunk to help give me a push.

"You're almost there, Lissa," Beck called out.

I tossed my hair out of my face and looked up at him. I was about halfway up, and I could feel my arms getting tired. Why do I let him talk me into these things?

"Beck, when I get up there, you better stay with me," I huffed.

Suddenly there was a scraping sound at my feet, and I was slipping, sliding down the tree. I screamed as the ground quickly grew closer. There was movement above me. I heard Beck yelling my name. He sounded closer. I landed on my side, hitting the ground with a loud thunk.

Beck jumped to the ground with me. He lightly touched my shoulder and asked if I hurt anything. He sounded worried.

I rolled over and saw wide brown eyes staring back at me. This wasn't the first time I failed to climb a tree, but it was the first time I saw him look so worried.

I quickly sat up and felt all over my body for cuts or blood. I could feel my eyes starting to burn with tears.

Beck started rambling words at me. "Alessia, I tried to get to you. You were falling so fast, and I knew you were closer to the ground, but I—I thought I could get to you! Are you okay?"

My scraped arms throbbed, but I waved my hand at his fussing. "It's okay. I think I'm alright." My voice wobbled, and tears trickled down my cheeks.

Beck stood up and offered his hand. "Hey, let's go get some ice cream?"

Ice cream always cheered me up.

I looked up at him. A small smile crossed his face. I reached out and grabbed his hand.

That was the day I knew Beck was someone in my life who cared if I was hurting and wanted to make it better.

I woke to tiny pieces of childhood memories flitting away like a tiny wisp: There but quickly vanishing beyond my reach.

I pulled on a pair of flannel drawstring pants and followed the tenor and baritone voices I heard harmonizing with the soundtrack to The Greatest Showman. They increased in volume with every step I took down to the kitchen. Beck, Ben, Conrad, and Thalia danced and navigated around each other as they prepared and cooked breakfast.

The boys goofed off more than actually making any progress. Singing along while making wild gestures with their hands and idiotic dance moves. The chorus hit, and to my surprise, Thalia turned around from the eggs she was cooking and joined them.

Reaching the bottom of the stairs, I paused and watched them. All of them smiling and laughing, a moment of togetherness and simply enjoying each other. Sweet and personal. Their shared connection as a family caused a surge of envy. I didn't have this in my life.

Beck spotted me, and his smile grew. He waved me over, offering me a seat on one of the island stools. A platter of sliced meats and cheeses sat in the middle of the counter, and a variety of bread options. Beck pushed a bowl of strawberries over so I could reach.

"Morning." He smiled. Causing my heart to do that stutter nonsense. *His smiles may be the death of me.*

"Mornin', Caramel." Ben winked and grabbed a strawberry, popping it in his mouth.

"Caramel?" I helped myself to a strawberry, too.

"Yeah, you remind me of it. You're sweet but also a little sticky. Because, let's face it, you have a permanent hold on this family."

"We sure we want to add a girl to the mix," Ryder said and sat beside me.

"Beck is," Ben said, laughing.

"Mornin' Mama T," Ryder greeted and ignored Ben.

Thalia was still humming to the tunes playing from the speaker.

"Morning Ryder." She turned around, spilling the scrambled eggs into a bowl on the island. "And good morning, Alessia. How did you sleep?" Her smile genuine and pleased to see me.

After Beck and I climbed back through the window, I fell fast asleep and slept deeper than I had in a long time.

164

"I slept great. Thank you for breakfast and, ya know, allowing me to stay here." Thank you didn't seem enough. No one spoke about it, but I sensed they risked a lot to have me here.

"Nonsense, dear. I do apologize for our meeting yesterday. It was a bit of a shock at first." She leaned closer, whispering, "But none of that is your fault." She passed me a knowing look like we shared a secret.

"Momma, look at this awesome toad I found," Jasper squealed. He came running in from outside, holding a massive toad.

"Oh, lovely, sweetie." Her face betrayed the excitement in her voice, but Jasper was too enthralled with his creature to notice. She ushered him back out the door, talking about finding the amphibian a home—outside. I smiled as I watched them; memories with my own mother swirled to the surface.

"I think I could get used to that." Beck moved a little closer to my seat, consuming my space.

"Used to what?" I asked, raising an eyebrow.

"That smile." Those brown eyes pierced me, and too many emotions fought to be first for me to know how to respond.

"Hey, probably should tell her about the hair dye. Oh, and how mom thinks she should probably cut it too," Ben said around a mouthful of food.

"Hair dye?" I asked.

"You know, to change your look. You're in hiding, right," Ryder said, reaching over me to grab some strawberries.

Mom suggested we make some changes to your hair to throw some doubt for anyone looking for you," Beck interjected. "It's just a precaution. Ben took care of covering our tracks. No one knows to even look for us here."

Ben flicked his fork at us. "That's not entirely true. The Order knows where we live. It wouldn't take too much detective work to put two and two together."

"It's fine. I could use something new anyway," I said. The idea growing on me.

"While Dad and her were out last night, Mom also picked up a few clothing items for you. I put them in the room," Beck said.

I finished breakfast and hopped off the stool to head upstairs. Beck said he would be up shortly, and we could work on my hair.

Walking into the bedroom, I saw several outfits, underwear, and socks lying on the bed. I changed into a pair of light-wash jeans and set aside a mustard yellow top and an oversized grey cardigan to put on after Beck finished with my hair.

I glanced around for a place to store the rest of the clothes. The closet door was slightly open. It was small inside, with some shirts, dress pants, and various jackets hanging up. Above that was a shelf the length of the closet. I moved a few items to make room for my small pile of clothes and noticed several shelves hidden by the shirts along the side.

A decorative dark walnut box inlaid with brass designs piqued my attention. It was beautiful, and I instantly became curious about what Beck might keep in such a delicate box.

I pulled it from the shelf, telling myself I just wanted to look at it.

Looking turned into opening.

Inside was a stack of envelopes. Some with my name on them and some with Beck's nickname for me—Lissa. *Why is he keeping a box of envelopes with my name on them?*

Curiosity won out.

I rushed to the bed and sat down, carefully pulling out the envelope on top and opening it.

It was a letter. He was responding to something I shared with him in one of my letters during the summer before Junior year—the last letter I sent him.

I grabbed the next one. This one was from my Sophomore year. He wrote about his family and some crazy antics for which he and his brothers got in trouble.

Another letter. Freshman year. A response to the first letter I wrote after moving. I felt the sorrow and sadness bleed into me with each word. He was hurt I was gone and would never be part of his life again.

I felt a tear slowly fall down my cheek.

I looked over at the box. So many letters. So many times he wrote me but never sent them.

Underneath the letters to me were envelopes with my handwriting, addressed to Beck. *He kept them.*

My chest tightened with an overwhelming feeling. A feeling of being wanted and loved.

Like I mattered.

Seen.

The bedroom door opened, and my head swiveled to see Beck standing there.

His eyes went to the letter in my hand before bouncing to the box. Hesitancy coated his walk as he entered the room.

"Why did you never send them?" I said just above a whisper.

He moved closer. Mouth opening and then closing. His eyes looked away.

"I wanted to. You have no idea how much I wanted to." His gaze returned to mine. "I convinced myself it was better for you to hate me than risk putting you in danger. My world isn't exactly safe," he said.

I stood, moving to close the distance between us.

"Why write back?" I whispered.

Our faces so close my heart beat with anticipation.

"It felt like in some way I was still a part of your life. In my mind, our conversations stayed alive, and so did my feelings for you."

I didn't think. Pushing up on my toes, I kissed him. A quick peck before I fell back and second-guessed myself.

But faster than I could blink, Beck's hands grasped me around the back of my neck and pulled me into him, our lips meeting. Lips, soft and warm, stroked. Fingers kneaded. The taste of strawberries teased at my tongue.

I've only ever been kissed one other time, on a stupid dare at a party.

But this.

Beck's hands traveled to my hips, pressing me even closer. My hands weaved into his hair as he deepened the kiss. Time stood still. I was falling, lost in the sensation. Lost in a moment with the boy who always made me feel found. Like I belonged.

Sometimes people come and go. But then some make such an impact they leave a mark on your soul.

Beck was that mark.

He squeezed at my waist as our lips barely parted.

His nose brushed my cheek. Our breathing mingled.

"You far surpass anything I ever could have imagined, Lissa." His eyes focused on me with a serious glint. "There is no turning back for me now. It's always been you. Since I met you, I knew there was something special about that girl who lived down the street. She drove me crazy and I couldn't get enough of her. She made everything else dim in comparison to her light. I was captivated by it. And now I will fight for it.

I could lose everything, Lissa. But I can't lose you. Not again."

His words ignited something inside of me I couldn't yet describe. But they broke me and healed me at the same time. Filled me with something I didn't even realize was missing.

Loud footsteps ran down the hallway, and Ben appeared in the doorway. Features torn and worried.

"You have to go, Beck. Dad got a tip of some suspicious activity—people asking questions about two teens traveling together. He wants you and Ryder to take her to the Belgium safe house."

Beck's hold around me tightened. A muscle in his jaw clenched. He glanced back at me before letting go and racing out the door.

Chapter 20

I stood in the middle of Beck's room, reeling from the rapid shift in the atmosphere. One minute, I was wrapped in strong arms, experiencing fire and elation. The next, I'm doused with ice and fears.

Ben followed Beck when he left, and neither gave me any indication of what I should do.

That annoying prickle of helplessness swelled in my chest. *Don't go there. Distract. We'll need clothes, right?*

I changed into the clothes I set aside and then grabbed the bag on the floor we had used from New York. I started with the clothes I had just put away and thought grabbing some things for Beck might be helpful.

Opening the second drawer down, I found rolled shirts and underwear. Who keeps their underwear with their shirts? Hm, he's a boxer brief guy. Not that kind of distraction, Alessia. Stop it. This is a serious situation.

"What are you doing?" mirth riddled Ryder's words.

The underwear dropped from my hands, and I fumbled for words. "Nothing—I mean...I was packing some clothes. Ben said we're leaving."

"We are." He was still smirking, and I wanted to slap it off his face. "I like your forethought. But we have to-go bags prepared for stuff like this. Good to grab stuff for you, though. We'll be leaving quickly. Beck said to get you downstairs." He nodded his head toward the stairs.

Tossing a few more items into the bag, I dashed out the door and down the steps. A whirl of activity met me when I reached the bottom of the stairs.

Thalia was instructing the boys to certain rooms of the house to collect items she needed. Beck was on the phone, pacing, his one hand clutched in his hair. I watched as Conrad and Ben darted off to separate rooms. Ryder grabbed the duffel from my hand and headed to the door.

"Alessia, listen to me," Thalia said, touching my shoulders. "I had hoped we would get more time together and figure things out. But life rarely goes as we planned. The boys are trained for situations like this, so stick close to them and follow their instructions. Marcus and I will be in touch."

"Thalia, I'm sorry. This whole thing...." I wasn't entirely sure what was happening, but it would separate Beck's family. None of this was good. And I felt like it was my fault.

"Don't. We live to protect, dear. It's what we do. I never like it when my boys are in danger or this close to a situation, but don't you fret about that. It's part of who we are." Her eyes shifted to Beck, and she seemed to be debating something.

"One more thing. When I met your mother and became friends, she was pregnant with you. Beck was only about a year old, and I didn't have the other boys yet. Still, Marcus and I had decided to pause our work in the organization and focus on our family, and we stayed in that neighborhood. Shortly after you were born, your mother came to me in a panic. She was terrified something would happen to you. She told me she had been hiding. She never revealed who. Her fear made me want to help; it seemed like the right thing to do. As the years passed, I watched for anything to be out of sorts, but nothing ever came of her concerns. After her accident, I told Marcus what I knew, and we were suspicious that there was something more to the accident. Nothing ever presented itself. When you moved, Beck and Ben's training was getting more intense, and we were negotiating to receive several security contracts. I pushed her concerns aside as a young mother's exaggerated fears for her new baby. Now, I have no proof any of this is related, but I've been part of this world too long to not notice puzzle pieces that have the potential to fit." Her hold on my shoulder tightened, and she glanced at Beck again. "And I'm sorry, Alessia. Beck was right. You needed us. Motherly love for my babies can sometimes cloud my judgment."

I swallowed because I had no idea what to say in response. *My mother went into hiding? People were looking for her?*

Beck hung up the phone and rushed over to us. "Mom, we have to go." He tugged at my arm, pulling me from her. Pausing, he drew closer to her. "I'm sorry, Mom. It wasn't supposed to go this way. Dad is on his way home." Beck's words were filled with regret.

She pressed her palm to his cheek. "Beck, my sweet Beckett. You are shaping into such a beautiful young man. We will be fine. We'll be in touch. Take care of her." Thalia glanced at me one last time, then moved away from us.

A tug at my arm again, and Beck directed us toward the black SUV outside the front door. Ryder was in the driver's seat, flicking his sunglasses up and down. He straightened when he saw us approach. Beck opened the back door for me and then walked to the back to close the hatch.

Ben flashed past my peripheral and joined Beck at the back of the car. He handed him a small phone.

"It's encrypted to allow me to send you files if needed. But listen, I really want to come with you guys. Please, Beck, let me come," Ben pleaded.

Beck placed both his hands on Ben's shoulders. "Mom needs you here. And I need you to have access to getting me more information so we can figure out our next plan of action."

Ben's head shook. "Fine, but don't do anything stupid without me," he said.

"Not a problem when all the stupid is here," Beck said, lifting the corner of his lip.

"Ha, okay," Ben said, shoving Beck's shoulder. "Seriously though, be careful."

"Don't worry, I will." Beck slapped Ben's back and smiled before Ben bounded back into the house.

Then Beck hopped in the front, and we sped down the long driveway. Leaving this home that I had only spent one day in but realized the family within it was quickly becoming something far greater to me.

⌾

Landscapes of fields, farmlands, and forests drifted by in quick motion. Little towns that looked straight out of a children's storybook. Castles nestled on small mountains. And the beginning stages of fall's vibrant colors were on bold display. It was a land of enchantment, with no time to enjoy it.

Several hours went by without a single stop. And as I watched the vast world passing by out the window, I recounted the events that brought me to this point in life. Events that have pushed me deeper into a world of unknowns. A life I didn't know how to handle.

Why were there people after me? When will I return home? Would I be able to talk to my dad soon? Was he okay? Who had my mother been hiding from? And why?

Falling into a pit of dread and anxiousness was inevitable. Secrets kept creeping into my life to the point I didn't know what or who to trust. My own mother held secrets so deep they were affecting me now. I wished she was here. She would have answers to calm my nervous heart and soothe my tangled thoughts.

The emotional storm that has been brewing for weeks cracked louder. Refused to be ignored.

Anytime anything has gone wrong, it's always been easier to bury it and focus on the next task.

The grief of losing Mom was too much to bear alone. Bury it. Seeing Beck again brought hurt feelings I thought I had let go. Distract. Dad's emotional absence was easier to deal with if I didn't address it. But now I don't have a task to focus on. I'm sitting in a car with nowhere else to turn. What am I going to do?

We finally stopped in a small town in Belgium that reminded me of a scene from a Renaissance-era movie. We exited the car and walked toward a small cafe. The sky was a perfect blue with white puffy clouds. Smells of sweet pastries drifted to my nose. Chatter from the people who filled the shops and cafes filled my ears. Despite the warm sunshine, the air was cool against my skin, and I wrapped my sweater tighter around me.

The cafe wasn't busy. One person was in line in front of a wrapped counter with a chalkboard menu behind it and freshly made goods inside the display case. And one person sat alone at a round table for two.

"I'm going to use the restroom," I said, walking past the ordering line.

Beck scanned the room. "I'll be right here," he said.

When I came out of the bathroom, I bumped into someone standing by its door.

"Oh, sorry. I don't know how I didn't see you there." My hands went up to brush the hair back from my face.

The guy I bumped into turned to look at me. His blonde hair was thick and wavy and hung by his ears. He was young, probably mid-20s. His blue eyes widened, followed by a smile. "American! Cann't say I've ran into many a ya folk in these parts. Nah ta biggest tourist track. You visitin' family?" he said with a strong accent.

How was I supposed to respond to that?

"I—um, no." I moved around him, but he bent in front of me.

"'Old up. Did ya drop this?" He held in his hand a gold bracelet. It was simple and had a couple charms on it.

"No, that's not—" I began.

"Can't leave you alone for a second, can I?" Fingers intertwined with mine. Beck's words were for me, but his eyes focused on the man holding the bracelet.

A smirk appeared on the blonde guy's face. "Ah, I see now."

A beat of silence passed as they continued to stare at each other. *Awkward.*

Beck pulled my hand, leading us away, but the guy moved, jostling me.

"Excus—" I was cut off by Beck tucking me closer to him and quickly advancing us toward the door. "We aren't getting food?" My feet tripped to keep up with his pace.

"There was recognition in his eyes. I don't like it. We need to leave. Now," Beck said.

"What about Ryder?"

"He'll be here," was all he said.

He pushed through the cafe door, and we stepped onto the sidewalk. Beck released my hand, walked to the vehicle, and opened the back door.

"Oy, where might we be off to sa fast?" I turned my head back toward the cafe. It was the blonde guy from inside, and he wasn't alone—two other men were with him.

A sense of foreboding struck.

Their presence was hostile, as if they meant us harm. But we were on a public street. *Would they really attempt something malicious toward us?*

Beck shoved me behind him. The blonde walked closer, shaking his head.

"It doesn't hav' to be complicated. Tel' ya what. We'll let ya live, and ya jus' give us the girl." He nodded toward me, a wicked grin filling his smooth face. "I'm bein' generous here." His hands extended out either side of him as if playing the innocent in this arrangement.

I grabbed Beck's shirt at the back of his shoulder. We needed to get in the car and leave.

"Yeah, she'll be going with us," Ryder confirmed and strolled behind them.

When I first met Ryder, I thought he was a friendly, wholesome jokester, but the guy staring down these three men before me was the furthest thing from being friendly. His stance predatory, and the intent in his gaze spoke of dangerous things. It hit me that Beck and Ryder were not your average 19-year-olds. I knew that. But something about seeing it play out in real time changed the reality.

The next movements around me happened so fast my eyes could barely keep track. The two men behind the blonde advanced on Ryder, but not before Ryder caught the arm of the first guy, twisting it backward, his fist colliding with the man's face. Bending the guy forward in half, he shoved him into the second man, causing them both to land hard on the ground.

At the same time, the blonde pounced toward Beck. My body was shoved further behind Beck, my elbows and back crashing into the SUV.

Beck blocked, his elbow connecting with the blonde's jaw. He bent, his hand slamming into the guy's leg, and busted his kneecap. A painful scream tore from his mouth before Beck released him. Then Beck's hands were on me, bringing me back from my fixation on the fight. He pushed me through the open SUV door and into the back seat, following me before he shut the door. Ryder jumped in the front, slamming his door at the same time.

"Go!" Beck yelled.

Ryder swore and got the car moving.

"That was too close." Beck glanced behind us as the car sped out of the little town onto a small road. "How did they find us?" Beck growled.

"This isn't good, Beck." Ryder eyed him in the rearview mirror. "Someone must be leaking information. You need to call your dad. The safe house may not be an option anymore."

"You're right." Beck swiped his hand down his face and pulled out the small phone Ben gave him. "You alright?" he asked me. His hand finding my cheek, and his touch centered my attention, helping me breathe through the adrenaline coursing in my veins. My heartbeat blared in my ears.

"Yeah, I think so," I breathed, my head doing a bobble thing. *I am so far from okay.*

"Don't worry, we'll get this figured out." His fingers moved my hair away from my cheek. He sounded so confident. But when my gaze caught Ryder's in the mirror, I didn't see the same confidence residing in his.

Chapter 21

Ryder drove us further along the winding roads, pulling us deeper into the wooded hillsides of Belgium. The greenery thick and dense. Trunks taller than me blurring by.

Beck called his dad to update him on the current situation. Marcus agreed the safe house we were headed to would no longer be an option and that someone close to them or within the Verndari organization was a possible mole.

As I listened to Beck and Ryder discuss what to do, the adrenaline from the fight waned, and instead, the weight of distressful emotions enclosed my thoughts.

My storm I'd been ignoring was about to open up like a torrential downpour.

I needed air.

"Stop the car!" I blurted. Two heads swiftly turned, giving me a surprised look.

"We're kind of on the run." Ryder tried to reason.

I couldn't respond, my inner panic taking over. I pinched the neck of my shirt, lifting it up and down to cool my overheated skin. Rubbing my sweaty palms along my leg, my eyes collided with Beck's.

He observed me for a moment and, without looking away, said, "Slow down so we can pull off up ahead."

"Beck, I don—" Ryder started.

"I said do it!" Beck's eyes darted to Ryder's in the mirror.

The vehicle slowed, and Ryder maneuvered us off the road.

My fingers fumbled with the door handle until it finally released, and I jumped out, walking a few feet into the wooded space.

Ripples of pinks, oranges, and purples blended on the horizon before me.

I ran my hands through my hair, inhaled a deep, slow breath, and counted to five before exhaling, but there wasn't enough air. My world tilted, and I swayed, stumbling. I crouched, resting on my heels to steady myself. My hands still braced on either side of my head.

"Lissa?" Beck approached me like one would a frightened animal.

"I can't do this. It's too much," I managed to get out between quick breaths.

"I know it's a lot," his voice was low and calm. "I know. And I know you're not used to this." He paused.

"I can't." My butt plopped to the ground. I pulled my knees toward me, placing my face between them as I tried to control my breathing. *Air. I need more air.*

Beck's footsteps drew closer.

Warmth from his hand seeped into my bones from the light touch on the center of my back. "This okay?" he asked.

My head did a slight nod.

"Yo, this is all really sweet, and I'm sorry you're struggling. But we gotta get out of here," Ryder yelled from his window.

"Park it in the woods. Just give us a minute," Beck hollered back, his hand still firm on my back. He moved closer to my ear, his voice lowering again. "I'm going to sit behind you, and I want you to match my breathing. Take very slow, deep breaths and listen to the sound of my voice."

He slid across the ground. Legs wrapped around either side of me, his arms enclosing to hold me against his chest.

"See that sunset? I want you to focus on only that. Forget we're in the woods. Forget Ryder waiting in the car. Listen to the sound of my voice. You're safe. Here in my arms, you're safe." Low rhythmic vibrations on my back, low and rhythmic. "Let your body feel warm, heavy, relaxed. Imagine that big old oak tree we used to climb together. Do you see it?"

Another small head nod. My breathing slowed, matching his.

"Hear the laughter. Feel the bark under your fingertips. Now, think back and remember what I told you. What I told you when you were scared and said you couldn't do it."

I could see it all. Beck was at the top of the tree laughing, telling me to face my fears and trust him, while I looked up, wondering how he got so high.

The steady rhythm of his heart beat against me, and mine met his in return. We sat there.

Breathing in and out.

Together. In tandem.

His arms pressed me into him. But then the memory of the tree continued, and I remembered falling and failing.

I leaned away in frustration. "Beck, no, I can't."

He moved in front of me, his hands resting on my shoulders. "You can. You don't have to keep hiding from it all, Lissa. I know the pain you've walked through. I was there before and am here now."

I sighed. "You told me to face my fears, and then I fell to the ground." I stood, pushing his arms aside, and he stood with me. "I'm not you, Beck. You always seem to know how to make things better, and I get scared or worried. I don't know what to do. Is my dad okay? Is he in danger? Am I going to spend the rest of my life on the run, always looking over my shoulder? Will the ache of loss and pain from my mom ever not nag at me? There are so many unknowns." Tears slid down my cheeks, and I crossed my arms as if to hold myself together.

He shook his head. "I know there are. I don't have this all figured out, either." His hands went wide on either side of him. "There are so many times I waver in doubts and fears. So many times, I want to take my family, those I care about, and give them a life without all this darkness. But we both know it doesn't work like that. We just....Sometimes in the dark, the darker it is, the easier it is to find the light. We just have to be willing to look for it."

"I don't know how. I don't know what I'm looking for," I cried.

"Each day presents us with new choices. We can't change the ones we made yesterday or the ones made for us. But today, we can keep pressing on despite the fears or the worries. Knowing each day matters. Because tomorrow, I want to see that smile on your face that lights up the room. And hear Ben laugh when he makes a stupid joke. I want to keep learning new skills from my parents. See Conrad finally make his slam dunk. It's connected, Alessia. We matter to each other, and we don't walk alone. I should have never let you feel like you had to." He moved closer, one hand placed on my shoulder, and the other lifted my chin. "I may not be able to change the world and how it works, but I know helping you will change my world." His hold melted into a hug, and his lips pressed against my hair as my eyes closed.

How did he keep doing that? How did he know the exact words needed to pierce my heart.

I wrapped my arms around him and clung to not only his hold but every sentiment in the words he had said. I wanted to take them and make them real. To solidify a truth that made a change. But I wasn't sure how.

Beck leaned back, eyebrows raised. "How we doing?"

I smiled and pinched my fingers together in front of him, showing a small amount. "We're at least moving in the right direction," I quipped.

After we climbed back into the SUV, the toll of my erratic emotions depleted me. Overwhelmed and spent, my eyes slowly closed and flickered open a few times as I lay against Beck's chest. His arm draped across me and pulled me in tight. His low timbre lulled me into a deep slumber.

∾

A cool breeze tickled across my exposed arm above the covers I was snuggled under. Peeking one eye open, my vision filled with beautiful French doors. One of the doors was swung open, leading to a small terrace, and white curtains swayed in the same breeze that cooled my skin while birds chirped happily in the glorious sunshine. I was in a large bed with white sheets and a honey-colored quilt. *Where am I?*

I pulled the blanket back and crawled out of bed, my feet hitting the cool amber tile flooring. Various types of rocks rendered tan tones along the walls. The cardigan I wore lay on a bench at the end of the bed, and I still had on the jeans and mustard top I had worn the day before. Curious about what was beyond the double doors, I walked over to the terrace, and my breath caught.

I've only seen pictures of Italy, but there was no mistaking the rolling hills with holm oak trees. Fields with beautiful pops of lavender, red, and yellow wildflowers. The terracotta roofing next to me covered a patio below. And a delicate olive tree hugged the terrace I stood on.

Soft humming and the clanging of silverware drifted up to me from the patio. Walking back through the small room, I opened the bedroom door to find a stone staircase that led down to the entranceway and a cozy kitchen. No one was in the kitchen, so I explored further and found Ryder passed out on a leather couch in the living space.

The same view as above greeted me through the large window behind the couch. Another door adjacent to the living room stood open.

Beck walked through, whistling. He stopped when he noticed me. A smile tugged at his lips. "You're awake," he said.

"Yeah. Where are we?"

Beck continued past me and entered the kitchen. "We are in the northern countryside of Italy. My grandparents on my dad's side were from here. They owned this land with a little villa on it. Remember I told you my family's legacy in the Verndari went back many generations?" Beck glanced at me, and I nodded. "This was their retirement plan. The home is secure from ever being connected to what we do. It was a long drive, but Dad said we would be safe here. It's too small to house all of us, or they would come too."

"Wow, it's beautiful." I observed the wooden cabinets and grey marble counters.

"I'd agree the view right now has increased its attractiveness." He grinned.

A coy smile lifted my lips.

"Hungry?" Beck grabbed some fruit from the fridge and wandered back to the door he came through, and I followed.

Outside was an adorable patio with a wooden table and chairs and a set of outdoor wicker seating around a fire pit.

An unobscured view of the hillside lay before us. *And I thought Germany was enchanting.*

"Is french toast still a favorite? We only grabbed a few items last night." Beck motioned toward the table, where a plate with food and two empty ones sat.

"It is. You made this for me?"

"It's yours now. I'll make some more." He pulled out the chair and nodded to the seat.

Oof, he's wreaking havoc on my heart.

If only this sweet moment could last forever, but apprehension to dream of such things still scared me because of the unknowns and the matter of deathly situations we found ourselves muddling through. I didn't know how to see past those obstacles and think we could be something more.

Something beautiful.

Even though, at this point, it would be impossible to remove Beck. He would always linger—in my thoughts, in my heart—no matter how the future played out.

"Thank you," I finally said and sat down.

Another smile, setting tingles ablaze. *Yeah, I will never get over him.*

Beck left to make more french toast, and I helped myself to an orange from the bowl he carried out.

He returned a little bit later, sitting beside me. Ryder still slept soundly on the other side of the wall.

"I think I believe you now," I said, finishing my last piece of toast.

Beck glanced over. "Believe me about what?"

"That you're some kind of secret spy guy."

He chuckled. "You're just now believing me? Everything that's happened so far and the fact you spot every time I'm hiding something didn't do it for ya?"

"No—that's not. Like, I believed you were telling the truth, but hearing something and then seeing something changes the perspective."

He took a sip of his water, eyeing me. "I'm not exactly a secret spy. My family, Mom and Dad, don't take espionage contracts or assassin work. Partly why they got so upset when I returned with you, and they learned of my involvement in one. But they used to do it all." He shrugged. "After they had a family, they held back. Wanted to be able to teach their kids and work together with them. I think limiting the jobs is a way of protecting us from the darker side of things. We mostly do joint security detail. Often for wealthy figures with threats against their lives. Sometimes political figures."

I fiddled with the hem of my shirt while I debated my next question. "Have you ever...I mean, have you killed people?" I whispered the last part, and my brows furrowed.

Beck frowned. "I have. A couple. To save the life of another." His head shook, and he cast his gaze out at the hills. "Doesn't make it easier," he admitted.

Our conversation suddenly felt heavy.

"Death is kind of like that," I pondered. "It takes. More than just the life of the dead person." I shook my head and looked away. "Life taught me a long time ago nothing lasts forever. We can wish it. We can crave it. But in the end, everything ends."

His eyes regarded me before he said, "True, but it also reveals to us the value of life and teaches us to embrace each moment with the time we have left."

His words struck hard, and I thought back on how vastly different my life looked in just a few days. How fickle time was.

We sat, both in silent thoughts. Beck's finger tapping on his knee.

Finally, I stood, gathering my plate. Beck rushed to stand and moved in front of me, grabbing my plate to set it back on the table.

I watched him, not sure what he was doing. His hand latched my hip and pulled me closer. The sizzle and crackle that was always there with his nearness kicked into overdrive, and my hands slid up his chest. He scanned my face before deep brown eyes finally met with mine.

"You don't have to fear it, Lissa. I know you still hurt and miss your mom, but not everyone who comes into your life will end the same way. There is still good in life worth fighting for. You get the honor of sharing her memory with the world. What she taught you and how she loved you. That's still a part of you and a part of her. You can still live with joy. We can still move forward without forgetting the path that brought us here. You can still remember her and let others in."

"You make it sound so easy."

"No, not easy. Hopeful," he said.

A smirk covered his mouth, and he pulled me further into him. "You said nothing lasts forever. But what if you let me be your nothing?"

I laughed. "Really? That's your line?"

Butterflies erupted deep in my belly despite the cheesiness.

With the most astonishing grin beaming on his face, his hand brushed my hair back.

"You can't really promise that, though," I whispered.

"No,"—he looked away, thoughtful, before returning his gaze to me—"but I can promise as long as I have breath in my lungs, there will never be anyone else but you for me. I will always be yours, Lissa. The world I'm part of is dangerous, and if something happened to you..."

His head bowed, and the hand around my waist fell. "I never realized how important you were to me until you left. It was why I let us drift. But maybe..." His eyes focused on me again.

His word *hopeful* bounced around in my head. An unspoken request loomed between us. His face entreating. Asking me to stand in the same hope he had.

The butterflies disappeared. He said he could lose everything, but not me. Not again. *What did that mean? That he wasn't afraid anymore?*

"Maybe not everyone will leave my life, but the hurt when the important ones do. I can't," my voice shook. There was no guarantee of any of it. And what if I couldn't handle losing him again.

Beck's face was torn between grief and frustration, his hand forming a fist. I turned from him and walked back into the house.

Chapter 22

We worked together cleaning up breakfast. Ryder woke to clear out the small amount of food we had, which left us needing more supplies. Beck decided to head to a nearby market to grab a few more things.

With nothing else to do, I hopped in the shower for some alone time. *My brain may slow down enough to finally think.*

While I indulged in the streams of hot water, my thoughts churned with the what-ifs and the reality I faced— things weren't going to become easier.

New obstacles would always present themselves, and I had two options: Face my fears and allow the journey to strengthen me, or run from them and become crippled by them. I wanted to face my fears, specifically the ones that kept me from letting others too close. But that terrified me. The thought overwhelmed. It made me want to hide so I didn't have to face the heartache of loss. *What might that achieve, though? How would I ever move forward if I chose to always stay hidden? How could I love or be loved?*

Afterward, I felt better; some of the fog in my brain had dissipated, and I could at least see the next step before me with clearness.

Beck hadn't returned yet when I came downstairs. I looked around the small kitchen and living room for Ryder before stepping outside. Just beyond the stone patio, Ryder was out in the grass doing burpees.

"Is this what you guys do with your downtime," I teased.

Ryder glanced up and gave me a broad smile. "This figure doesn't build on its own. Plus, just keeping up with your boy." He winked.

I scrunched my nose. "My boy? I don't know if—"

"Oh, don't even deny it. Beck is one of the best I've worked with. He's level-headed and the guy you want watching your six. But since you've shown up,"—he shook his head, smiling—"his focus is a little...distracted."

A distraction? Was that good or bad?

"I didn't...I mean, I didn't even know...." I trailed off.

Ryder offered a sympathetic smile. "It's okay. It's not necessarily a bad thing."

His hands went to his hips, and his gaze took in the view around us. When his eyes returned to me, he said, "He's just worried, ya know? Although, I have an idea that could be helpful. Particularly if we find ourselves in another tussle like yesterday." He waved his hand, motioning for me to come closer. I obliged.

"Ever taken any self-defense classes?" he asked.

"No."

"Well, I've been told I'm an excellent teacher."

A half-hour later, Ryder's arms circled around me from behind for the fiftieth time, securing his fake attack. "Now, I want you to press as hard as you can this time with your thumb here,"—he pointed to the front of his thigh—"on the sciatic nerve, twist and thrust your palm into my jaw. And once I release, you're free to run."

My attempts so far to free myself from Ryder's hold proved to be complete failures. I had my doubts this one would be any different.

"Okay, but what if I hurt you?" I asked, and I could practically hear his eyes rolling.

"Doubtful. And if you do, that's progress."

I did as he said, pressing my thumb into his leg as hard as I could. His leg quivered, and his arms loosened, freeing me enough to twist and shove my hand with force into his jaw. But my movements were timid and hesitant, and his head barely moved from the impact. His arms gave way, and I stared as he rubbed his jaw.

"Better." He chuckled.

"Honest?" I was more than a little skeptical.

"Yeah, I felt that one a bit." He continued to rub his jaw.

"Sorry."

A throat cleared from the direction of the house, and my head spun to see Beck leaning against the doorframe, looking slightly amused and annoyed. Ryder nodded and went back to giving me instructions.

"Alright, we're going to try—"

"Hey Ryder, think you need a break?" Beck still stood against the frame, arms crossed.

Ryder straightened and winked at me before hollering back, "I'm good, man. Just getting warmed up. She caught me good on that last one."

Beck pushed off the door and strolled over to us.

"Did I say worried? I meant territorial." Ryder grinned, and Beck positioned himself next to him.

"What have you practiced?" Beck asked.

"Basic snatch and release."

Basic? There was nothing basic about what Ryder was teaching me. I watched them as they conversed back and forth about me.

"Hey! I'm standing right here." I waved my hands in front of me to draw their attention.

"Trust me, we're well aware." The side of Beck's mouth lifted. I crossed my arms. *Punk.*

"Okay. Your goal isn't to fight the attacker but to fight the attacker's objective," Beck instructed, his words firm and proficient."When they grab you, they want to take control. You, as the victim, have to put yourself in control. You need to control what happens next." He grabbed my wrist, jerking me into him. "Take control back."

I blinked, confused. So caught off guard, I just stared at him. He released me and moved back. He grabbed my wrist again, and I jerked forward again.

Annoyed, I huffed. "Are you at least going to show me what I need to do?"

He leaned in. His nose grazed my forehead. "Take control."

I don't think I'm meant to feel a warmth in my belly from that.

He let go and moved away again. Ryder also backed away.

When Beck grabbed my wrist the next time, I knew it was coming, and I didn't jerk forward. As much. Instead, I pushed against his pull with my other hand and thought about how to take control of the situation. *Think, Alessia. Think.*

I pushed against his hand and tugged at my arm, trying to free it. He easily yanked me into him, and I bounced off his chest.

"You're fighting against it. Take control," he whispered, his lips brushing my cheek.

"I'm beginning to think you just like having me close to you." I smiled as I looked up at him.

He shrugged and moved back. "Think, Lissa. How can you control my arm?"

Once again, he grabbed my wrist. I instantly placed my opposite hand on his, but he pulled me into him again. I shoved him back this time. "A hint, perhaps?" I spouted.

His response was in action. He grabbed my wrist, brown eyes focused on me.

Okay, pushing and pulling don't work. He said I'm fighting against it. But what if I...

Placing my other hand over his, I swung the arm he was holding upward, twisting his arm as I went. Then I grabbed his wrist with the hand he was holding. In doing so, the new angle of his arm held him locked, and I regained control of my wrist.

Ryder came up between us. "Well done. See, in this position, he's now at your mercy once you apply pressure, causing him to fall. Watch." Ryder applied more weight to my hand, and Beck fell to his knee, his arm twisted further, and his back angled toward us. A slight breath of air escaped him. "He can't stand up, even if he tried."

I jumped back. A thrill ran through me. *I did it!*

Beck returned to his feet and smiled at me. "Now you know you can take control."

I squished my lips together and to the side. "Is that why you didn't just tell me what to do?"

"That, and I liked watching that cute look on your face every time you got frustrated."

I pushed him away, but he caught my arms and pulled me close. "It's important you know you can do it and know how to think through it. And not just in a physical fight, but the battle you fight in here," he said, pressing two fingers to my temple.

"Thank you."

His responding boyish smile warmed me.

"We'll work on muscle memory later."

His phone rang from his pocket, breaking the moment, and Beck pulled it out to answer.

"Yeah?" he answered.

Someone spoke on the other end, and Beck moved away from me toward the house. Ryder and I followed.

When we entered the living room, Beck set up a laptop on the coffee table and placed the phone on speaker.

I sat down next to him, and Ryder sat on the other side of the coffee table.

"I've been digging deeper into the Dufort investments and if Alessia's dad has any connections. Oliver Weber was requested for consideration at Ridgecrest by Lyle Dufort just over three years ago. Back when he received the job there. And he and Alessia moved." Ben's voice came through the phone.

"Wait. Lyle requested my dad for the job at Ridgecrest?" I thought back to Lyle's comment at the benefit and excitedly patted Beck's leg. "Beck, Lyle said at the benefit that he had met with my dad a few times."

Beck sat forward. "Did he say why? Or hint at it relating to business or something more?"

"No, that was all he said. But these two things connect, right?"

"Does look awfully shady," Ryder added. "It proves that Lyle has a connection with your dad and holds some piece of value for him."

"Unfortunately, I haven't found any other hints of their relationship outside the school," Ben said. "I also did as you asked and checked on Oliver in Japan. He's still in the hospital. Records indicate a few more days before he will be released."

My hand squeezed Beck's leg. Silently thanking him for checking in on my dad.

"However, I didn't trust just following some digital footprint," Ben said. "I tapped into the hospital's surveillance footage to see what might be going on. I couldn't see in the room, but I did pick up on some odd activity. Two men visit daily and sometimes just hang out in the hall outside his room."

Beck and I looked at each other. Concern for my dad's safety took hold of my heart and gripped like a vice.

"What does that mean? Why are men watching him?" I asked Beck, but Ben answered.

"I can try to get older footage to see how long they have been visiting. But my guess is the visits correlate to when Beck pulled you from the States."

"Can I contact him? Talk to him? Maybe he can help us." My words fumbled out with panic. Dad was alone and could be in trouble.

Beck shook his head. "I'm not risking revealing where you are. We have no secure way of reaching him. Ben can continue to keep an eye on him and give us feedback. So far, he's safe."

"Beck, that can change at any second. We just realized he knows Lyle Dufort and never told me. Our relationship isn't exactly close, but why would he never mention a partner of a massive company like Vasili Inc. requested him for a job at Ridgecrest. He'd be giddy over the idea," I argued. "And it was the school who sent him to Japan. Was that on Lyle's request, too? And these strange men outside his room. What if his fall at the airport wasn't even an accident?"

"Okay, slow down. We've established there is a connection between your dad and Dufort. But we still haven't confirmed that it's Lyle Dufort behind the contract through the Verndari," Beck said.

"But we're close, Beck. It's gotta be somebody connected with this school or her dad. It fits too well to not be," Ryder said. "Here's what we do know: That Tristan dude was involved, so they are connected to him somehow. The person knows of the Verndari, which means they have power. They know the ins and outs of the school and exactly where her dad is. With these new connections between her dad and this Lyle guy....I don't know something ain't smelling right about him."

"I agree it's a good lead, but it's not concrete enough. And it doesn't give us a solution," Beck said

"Enough to keep digging further," Ben's eager voice said.

"Yeah, Ben. Go hard at this. Look into any correspondence between Weber and Dufort in the last three years. It may be hard to find anything that far back. But I have a hunch this guy likes to hold on to things for his own leverage. Also, keep us posted on movement in Japan," Beck ordered. "Any updates on who is tracking our movements?"

"Will do. Dad's working on looking into those within the Verndari who know our routes and safe houses. That's helpful because that's a limited number, but I haven't looked further into that. I'll be in touch. Later." Ben hung up from his side.

"What if he's worried about me, Beck? I can't just sit here and leave him thinking something bad has happened to me. What if the school called him. I've been gone four days at this point. And Ava is definitely losing it." I understood Beck's view, but it was a frustrating one. It made me uncomfortable to not reassure them I was okay.

"I watched how Tristan operated with the school. Trust me, the school is keeping most of this under wraps. Just like they did with your attack in the locker room. They don't want to jeopardize their good name, and Tristan knows how to use his name to make situations work in his favor. If your dad has heard anything, it's due to his connection with Dufort. As for Ava,"—he sighed—"we're going to have to let her sit in the dark a little bit longer."

I didn't like it, and disappointment trickled in. I tried to reconcile Beck's reasoning, but leaving Dad and Ava to so many unknowns left me uneasy. "We can't send an anonymous message somehow?" I asked, eager for a crumb of hope.

"I'm sorry. I don't see a way until we get the upper hand on the situation and know more about what's happening. Digital messages are easily tracked, and we don't know what Tristan may have told her."

We sat in a beat of silence.

"I say, how about gelato for lunch?" Ryder stood, smiling, and effectively shifted the mood.

"Like going out?" I asked

Beck hesitated.

"We'll stay local. The girl needs some fresh air, Beck."

We hopped in the SUV and drove to a small town not too far away.

After parking, we wandered the narrow roads. A dazzling world of charm and wonder. Life was buzzing all around. A small boy chased a ball crossing our path on the cobbled street nestled between narrow, aged buildings while two old men sat smoking their pipes, and an english cream retriever rested at their feet.

Fresh laundry flapped across the sky above us, and bold notes of coffee smelled so strong I could practically taste them. All of it made it so easy to get swept away by the beauty oozing from every corner. Like I could forget for just a moment.

For a moment, I could be carefree. Pretend my life wasn't an out-of-control train heading for a collapsed bridge. And not try to riddle out the mystery of how it got there.

Perhaps envision my life to be something more magical. A life where I was on an adventure of exploring new and far places, and I was with Beck. My best friend, who I always saw as that—a friend.

Until that last summer before I moved. That was the summer life filled me every time I saw him. When I touched him. And I realized no one supported me like Beck. No one knew me like Beck.

Maybe it was love, too hard to tell when we were so young. But that life he charged me with never left.

The look in his eyes when he gazed at me, the charm in his voice when he asked to be my forever, and the fervor he has to fight for me told me there was more there for him, too.

I tried imagining how I would go back to life without him. I couldn't. But I've hidden myself for so long out of fearing the pain of loss. If I stepped beyond that...*would I survive the outcome?*

We stopped at a small cafe along a river where the gelato was melt-in-your-mouth perfection. I knew the answers for the future were unknown. But, as we sat together and I watched a more burden-free Beck laugh and tease me, I realized how much I needed his solid strength. He was everything I wasn't, and his strength filled me, lifting me to be stronger. *How did I not see I was lost without it?*

Chapter 23

The next few days, our time was spent mostly, if not all, at the house. Beck and Ryder taught me more defense techniques and drilled me until my muscles were so sore I could barely move. Each day intensified the weight of sitting in a brutal game of unraveling the mystery of someone wanting me dead. And I was no closer to solving it.

I sat outside on the terrace Friday morning, sipping on a Caffe cappuccino made by Beck himself, and it hit me that it had been a week since that whirlwind of a night with Tristan at the benefit. Unwillingly, flashbacks emerged from that evening, and I shuttered. With shaking hands, I set the cup on the small drink table.

Words resurfaced as I tried to reign in my thoughts. *"You know, someone went through a lot of trouble to hide you, Butterfly."*

I completely forgot he had said that. What did he mean someone hid me? And was that connected to what Thalia told me? My mom had gone into hiding. For how long? Why? From whom?

Maybe Beck and I could talk it out and come up with some ideas.

I tipped the cup, swallowing the last of my coffee, and stood, pressing pause on the endless stream of thoughts relating to the massive conundrum that was my life.

A breeze swept by, and I pulled my cardigan closer to my chest, causing the weight of something to shift in the pocket. I placed my hand inside and pulled out a gold charm bracelet. This wasn't mine. Why was it in my pocket? It looked familiar, but I couldn't place why.

I walked into the room, intent on going to the kitchen to show Beck, but a bouquet of bright flowers stole my attention.

A white vase with wildflowers was on the nightstand next to the bed. Lily like white flowers and lavender boasted, bold mustard sunflowers and red poppies accented, and leafy eucalyptus played a lovely mint, pulling the whole piece together.

A smile seized my face.

I stepped closer, set the bracelet on the stand, and ran my hand up one of the stems. My fingers caressed the soft petals. There was no note, but there were only two other people in this house, and one of them had a strong liking for me.

I hurried down the steps and found Beck washing dishes in the kitchen. I snuck up behind him, tapped him on the shoulder opposite where I stood, and hopped onto the counter next to the sink. His head swung directly at me, didn't even glance the other way. *Yeah, should have known that wouldn't work.*

"I heard you before you even reached the staircase," he said.

My shoulders scrunched against my neck, eyes squinting, and I leaned forward. "How?"

He grabbed a hand towel by my leg, drying his hands. "It's called being aware of your surroundings." He stepped closer, placing a hand on either side of me. "And it's been a fun pastime developing the habit of always being aware of where you are."

Pretending to be annoyed, I slid off the counter, his arms still trapping me. My hand skated up his chest and I shoved him. He laughed and allowed himself to fall back. But with lightning speed, he grabbed my waist and pressed me back against the edge of the counter. A happy grin lighting up his face.

A tiny breath escaped me at the sudden proximity.

"As fun as that pastime is, I can think of one that exceeds it," he alluded.

I tilted my head, angling my eyes up at him. "Found some flowers in my room. You wouldn't happen to know how they got there, would you?"

"I'm guessing someone gave them to you."

"Well, whoever did, that was very sweet of them."

"Not every day someone turns 18," he said.

It was the last day of September—my birthday. Bittersweet emotion captured the moment, and I thought of Dad. Every year, he would take the day off and do whatever I wanted to do for the day. *I missed him. Would I ever see him again?*

Beck's hand lifted, teasing at my hair. "Hey, everything okay?" he asked. His eyes softened from their playful spark.

I cleared my throat. "Just thinking about Dad. Anyway, that was thoughtful of you. Thank you."

"We're gonna work this out. Once we know why you're in danger and end it, I will find a way to reunite you and your dad. This isn't how it's always going to be."

Lifting up, I wrapped my arms around his neck and pulled him close. "Thank you for fighting for me," I whispered.

I angled my head back. His eyes drifted to my mouth, and a hand gripped my hip.

The temperature climbed by 30 degrees. And all I could think of was that moment in his bedroom. Where his lips

200

met mine in the perfect way, and everything felt right. His warm hands when they grabbed...

"Got some wood! I'm making a fire tonight," Ryder announced as he traipsed through the house entrance.

I released a frustrated breath. *I was about to make some fire, too, Ryder.*

"That sounds amazing. I love campfires," I said, eyeing Beck. I pushed against his chest to move past him and headed to the little bookcase in the living room. Getting lost in the pages of another time and place sounded like a good way to spend a lazy afternoon. *And not think too hard about the words—"I was there before and am here now."*

∽

Later that night, we sat on the patio around proof of Ryder's amazing fire skills. Mesmerizing and warm, the flames flickered bright, popping and crackling, but the air had a chill. I wrapped myself tighter in my blanket while I laid across the sofa, resting against Beck, who sat on the end. His hand lifted mine, and fingers danced and tickled against my palm.

"No, not all our work is high intensity. There was one time Ryder and I had a position as bouncers." Beck's chuckle vibrated against my back. "The owner said someone was sending him death threats. Going in as bouncers was an easy way to get in his circles without being noticed. Turned out his life wasn't in danger, just a pissed-off ex-wife."

"Well...maybe his life was in danger." Ryder laughed as he stoked the fire and reached for another log. "Gah, I hated that club. New York was a beast," he said, shaking his head.

"So, how does it work? You pick and choose from a list of contracts?" I asked, curious about the life they lived.

Beck's fingers ran up to the tips of mine and back down. "Sort of. It's a bit more complicated than that. There's a digital ledger of transactions on a blockchain. Basically a secure and decentralized storing and management of smart contracts. On the blockchain, clients can create a contract containing all the terms and conditions of the work, timeline, and payment terms for anyone connected to the network. In our case—The Verndari. They sort through which contracts fit our skill sets; from there, they post or assign it within our organization's network."

"So, yeah, we pick and choose from a list of contracts." Ryder joked before adding, "Gotta take a leak." He hopped up and went inside.

I sat up and turned, facing Beck. "Still no word from Ben or your family?"

"Mom checked in, but she was just being a mom. Checking in on me. And you, she wanted to make sure you were okay," he said.

"Aw, that was really sweet of her."

"Yeah, she's a pretty amazing woman."

His eyes caught with mine before drifting lower. He quickly looked away, and his hand rubbed the back of his neck. "I've missed you, Lissa. I had no idea how much until these last few days with you."

"Is that so? Well, I didn't miss you at all."

He laughed. "Right, that's why I have a box full of letters from you back at my parent's house."

The smile on my face grew, and I shoved his shoulder. His hand flew up to grab mine. Holding it, he said, "I know I shouldn't, but I want this,"—he waved his other hand between us—"I don't know how to give up on something that I now know is everything I want."

I swallowed and watched his fingers intertwine with mine. "Do you think that's possible? That we could actually be together." I've wanted to be with him since I was 14, but wanting something and being able to take hold of it are two different things. I brought my eyes in line with his. "I'm scared, Beck. How do I know I won't lose you?"

His body shifted, reaching over, his hand wrapped around the nape of my neck, his thumb rubbing my cheek. "If something is worth fighting for, shouldn't we fight for it?"

If he only knew how much of me was already his. I simply didn't know how to take that final leap into the unknown.

He dropped a light kiss near my temple. "We don't have to decide anything today. I'm going to go grab a hoodie. Be right back."

As he walked away, I noticed the warmth of his presence fade in more ways than I was ready to acknowledge.

I sat alone, watching the flames bounce in the fire. When a sudden presence appeared next to the fire ring and sat in the chair next to mine.

I looked up and saw Chelsea, coily locks flowing freely. She grabbed my wrist."Alessia. I'm so glad I finally found you. Please hear me out. It's not safe for you to be with Beck. The hit on him has gotten out of control, and you would be better off with someone Tristan isn't looking for. I have enough connections we can get you hidden. A new name, with a new life. Somewhere safe." Her words were low and rushed.

I was so shocked by her appearance that it took me a moment to register what she was actually saying. "What— What are you doing here? Wha—" A clicking sound to my right turned our heads in that direction.

"Alessia, come inside the house," Beck rumbled. He stood at the door with a handgun pointed directly at Chelsea.

There was a significant spike in my heart rate. *What is happening?*

Chelsea stood, tossing a smug look toward Beck. "Beckett, so drastic. I thought we were friends."

"You shouldn't have been able to find us. So that tells me one of two things. You're the mole who leaked our safe house route and somehow tracked us, or you've somehow hacked my brother's encryption skills. My bet is on the former. " He moved a little closer to me. "Alessia, I said, move inside."

My body finally caught up with what my mind knew. I hurried to move behind Beck, but not before Chelsea grabbed my arm and pulled me against her, my back hitting her chest.

Beck stepped forward, his grip on the gun tightened. "Victoria, I swear I will shoot. And I won't miss."

Victoria? *Oh, I forgot Chelsea is an alias.*

"Don't be silly, Beckett. She wants to come with me. She should really be more careful about taking jewelry from strangers, though." Chelsea tugged me tighter against her.

My eyes squeezed shut. I completely forgot to tell Beck I found that bracelet in my pocket.

"She and I were just chatting about how she would be safer with me. You think those three guys that showed up in Belgium were all you needed to worry about?" Her tongue clicked. "And poor, sweet Ava misses her."

I didn't know what to do. If I fought to get free, would Victoria have a weapon? The boys had been training me on defense tactics all week, but it was a far different feeling when real danger threatened me.

But Beck was right there. Ready. I went with my gut. I pressed on her leg with my thumb, and she yelped. I didn't even have time to twist because Beck's hand pulled me away and pushed me behind him into Ryder.

A female cackle sounded across the patio. "Do you really think I would come alone?"

Two men walked out of the shadows on either side of her. "I paid my favor, Beckett. I owe you no loyalty. But since you've been hiding here and most likely don't know, I'll share some updates. The price for the girl has gone up, and I always go where the money is. You know that. It's nothing personal, dear. You've clearly grown too attached."

"The Verndari are loyal, especially to their own. You're the one breaking codes. But that's always been a struggle for you, hasn't it," Beck said. He started backing up towards Ryder and me.

"I was only going to take her. No reason to cause bad blood within the Verndari. But if you're going to put up a fight, I'll simply have to remove the problem."

"Get her to the car, Ryder," Beck growled.

Ryder didn't hesitate. At a rapid pace, he moved me to the opposite side of the house to the SUV in the driveway just outside. *No, we can't leave Beck.*

He tossed me in the back seat and climbed in the front.

"Ryder, we're not leaving him! He wouldn't even be in this mess if it wasn't for me." I pulled the handle, but it was locked.

"Have a little faith," he retorted.

I gaped at him. "Ryder—"

His hand smacked against the dashboard. "They've disabled the car," he yelled, adding a slew of curses. He flung open his door and grabbed the handle of mine, pulling me from the backseat. "We have to find their vehicle. Come on."

Moving to the back of the SUV, Ryder lifted a hidden compartment under the seats and grabbed a black bag.

Gunfire sounded.

No.

I started running toward the house, but Ryder's arm latched around my waist, lifting me off the ground.

"Ryder, let me go. We have to help him!" My legs kicked against his shins while my hands pushed at his hold.

"Beck said to get you out. That's what I'm doing."

He moved us back over to the other side of the SUV, shielding us from view, while his head turned in several directions, looking for something.

I squirmed, trying and failing to free myself. Panic overrode; my only awareness was getting to Beck before it was too late.

"There it is," Ryder mumbled.

Someone skidded around the back of the car, and I was flung behind Ryder so fast my head was spinning. The bag hit the ground, and his arms sprang out in front of him, revealing a gun. *Where did that come from?*

"Whoa, it's me." Beck's voice was the sweetest sound to my ears. I shoved Ryder out of the way and ran into Beck, my arms squeezing him in a tight hug. I pressed my cheek into his chest, savoring the feel of his heartbeat. *He's okay.*

"Our way out is at the end of the drive," Ryder said, picking up the black bag.

Beck took my hand and raced us down the lane to the other vehicle.

Chapter 24

"**K**eep driving north. Get out of the country and into France. I'll call Dad. He'll need updating and be able to deal with Victoria from the inside," Beck said. Gruff and rushed. His breathing sharp.

I could relate. My heart was on the verge of exploding.

I reached for him, snatching his arm. "Beck. Beck, are you okay? Why did you stay there? That—that was the scariest thing I've ever...."

His hand landed over mine. "I'm not going to let anything happen to you. We have the means to get you to a new location. I just need a minute to figure out the next step," he said.

"No, not for me, Beck. For you! I was terrified for you. I heard that gunshot...." I pulled my hand back from him, fretting my fingers.

He reached for me again, leaning over the console, his hand rested against my ear. "Hey, hey. I'm fine. The gunfire was me. To give me enough time to get away and to slow them down."

I nodded, my nerves calming slightly with his reassurance.

Beck made a low rumbling sound. "That woman is like poison. That's not the Verndari way. She shouldn't have been able to find us," Beck stated, anger coating his words.

"It's not necessarily kosher to underhand another Verndari's contract either," Ryder added.

Beck's head whipped in his direction. "Who's side are you on, Ryder?"

"Of course I'm on yours. But you ain't exactly playing by the rules here. The world isn't a perfect black-and-white picture; everything doesn't always make sense. That's all I'm saying."

Quietness settled, and Beck stared out the window, still visibly upset.

His phone rang, and he pulled it from his pocket. Incoherent chatter flowed from the other side of the phone.

"Hold on, slow down. Who's moving?" Beck nodded, listening. "Yeah, well, things aren't going so great here, either. We just had a run-in with another Verndari, Victoria, who was the original contact on Alessia's contract. No, we're on the move. We'll need a place off the Verndari networks. Okay, I'll be in touch."

He hung up, tossing the phone into the center, and slammed a hand into the front dash. I jumped.

"Who was that?" I asked.

"It was Ben. He said your dad is leaving the hospital with the two men we saw watching his room."

"What? What does that mean?" Panic erupted. Wild and intense.

"She lost her trail on us. They're switching tactics," Ryder said.

Beck clenched his fist. "We'll have to find out where they are taking him."

"She? They? What are you talking about?" I asked.

"Victoria no longer knows our next move. Your dad is being moved before his release and with these men that have been there. The two incidents are linked. And since they no longer have a guarantee with you, they are going straight for your dad," Beck explained.

208

"It's desperate," Ryder said.

"But how to find which way they went," Beck muttered.

"What? How do you know they are linked?" I butted in.

"We evaluate the situations and learn from behavior. We've uncovered a connection between Dufort and your dad and the school. He leaves for a fancy trip, and suddenly, you have someone trying to murder you using an elite secret group. That shows they were willing to spend a lot of money to have it done quietly and with discretion. Then, when that backfires, men are staking out your dad's hospital room. That tells us they're willing to go to extreme levels to protect their dirt. Take my word for it. These aren't all coincidences, and this behavior fits a guy like Dufort to a T," Ryder said.

I nodded. The picture becoming clearer. "Then Tristan and him knowing what he knew would add further ties to his dad? How do we know it's not someone else involved with the school?" I asked.

"The probability is low. Adding Tristan's involvement and Lyle specifically requesting your dad and his status as a Dufort leaves an awfully big spotlight," Beck added.

All the pieces seemed to fit. But what if we were missing something? It all made sense, but maybe that was the problem. If all these pieces weren't coincidences, then there was a good chance my mom hiding herself played a part.

"Beck, what if it's not about my dad, and it *has* been about me? Thalia told me my mom went into hiding before she met my dad. She was still in hiding when she died. Tristan said they were looking for a dead woman and that someone had gone to a lot of trouble to hide *me*. Beck, I think they're going to use my dad to get to me."

"Talk about dropping a grenade. Geez, Alessia," Ryder said.

"Your mom was in hiding? And you? Why are you just telling me this now?" Beck twisted to face me. Hurt and stunned.

I grabbed his arm. "I'm sorry. I just remembered earlier today something Tristan said. And then all that stuff with Chels—sorry, Victoria, happened. But I feel like it's an important piece. We have to go back to Ridgecrest! To Connecticut," I urged.

I couldn't let him be in danger and not try to help. I didn't know what we would do, but I knew hiding wouldn't fix it.

"No! Absolutely not, Alessia. That would be playing right into their hand," Beck argued back.

I straightened. I knew this was his fear for me, and I was afraid, too. But it wasn't just my life on the line. Beck, my dad, Ava, and anyone else who may try to protect me were in danger. We couldn't keep on like this while they were at risk.

I wanted to shout back at him and argue, but that would only lead us in circles. Instead, I took a deep breath and slowly began to speak, "None of this is an ideal situation. Continuing to hide me will put the only family I have left in danger. Beck, you always pushed me to face my fears. You helped me to keep pushing forward, even when it was hard. And you're still doing it. You're scared, I know. I'm scared. But staying in our fears prevents us from experiencing the present. Experiencing the joy of those we still have time with. I'm more scared of a life without them. A life without you. I don't think we will have either if we keep running from this."

Beck stared at me.

A low whistle left Ryder's lips.

Beck's hand reached for mine, and a sad smile spread across his lips. "No, I don't like it. All I've ever wanted is to support you and see you grow into the amazing person I've always known you to be. You're right; we can't keep hiding, but..."

I leaned forward between the seats onto the center console, my fingers slipped into his hair at the nape of his neck, and I locked his eyes with mine. "Better together?"

Surprise crossed his face, and he looked down at our hands before his eyes returned to mine. "I will always be better with you. You make everything in life better, Lissa."

Soft lips slammed into mine.

Fingers slid to my neck, anchoring. Demanding more.

And I matched him. Creating the perfect rhythm. Unable to tell where I ended, and Beck began.

He pulled away too soon, but it did its job. His kiss told me all the things he didn't say. *Beck was with me.*

"Better together," he whispered.

We were on a flight en route to New York several hours later. Before departing, Beck filled in his family on our plan.

Or the lack of one.

Marcus and Thalia weren't surprised by our new direction. They didn't try to convince us to stay. Instead, they shared valuable tips. Scenarios for us to consider and what to expect if things go south. Marcus also planned to make arrangements to meet us in the States.

After landing, we rented a car, and Beck drove to the same storage unit we stopped at before. Beck and Ryder loaded the trunk with all sorts of equipment and weapons I'd never even seen before.

We didn't know where Dad was or if he was even here. We planned to set up my house as a secure base and observe the situation while calculating our next move. But we anticipated

Dufort's awareness of my arrival. And then we would wait. Wait for Beck's dad and Dufort's next move.

We reached the wooded lands behind my house with only a few hours till sunrise. We still had enough darkness we could remain hidden.

Beck parked the car, hiding it behind some heavy bushes. "Stay here," Beck said.

I rolled my eyes and followed them out of the car to a covered spot behind bushes and trees.

Beck watched me and shook his head. "Yeah, I don't know why I said anything," he whispered.

"There's no danger here. Why would I sit in the car and watch you?'

"Can I sit in the car?" Ryder huffed and covered his eyes with a pair of night vision binoculars.

From our position, we could see my street. The house was dark and quiet.

"I'm not seeing any movement. Do these have a heat sensor option?" Ryder inquired.

Beck nodded and clicked a knob on the binoculars. Ryder positioned them back on his face.

"We're clear. Are you coming with me or staying here?" Ryder slapped the back of his fingers against Beck.

"What, and leave me out here? Alone?" I said, bewildered.

"You're a bit of a liability inside; we'll move smoother and more efficiently if you're not there," Ryder said sternly.

I somewhat agreed he had a point, but I was still unhappy about it.

Beck shushed our argument and glanced at me. Uncertain.

"We don't know what we are walking into. I think Ryder is right. Stay low in the car out of sight, lock it, and we'll be in and out in less than 10 minutes."

I huffed. "I don't like it."

"I don't like it either, but I like it better than you being in or near the house while we attempt to gain the upper hand."

"And if you don't come back?" I whispered—because, yes, we were facing it, but I was still wrestling with fears.

Ryder chuckled, and Beck smirked as his arm came to rest on my shoulder.

"We have the luxury of surprise and are on offense now. You've only seen us on the defense. But it appears the house is clear. This is just a precaution. We'll come back." He winked and led me to the car.

"You doing okay?" he asked.

"Just come back, okay. Quickly."

"You can count on it."

Then he leaned in, his lips caressing mine in a quick and gentle slide of the lips, but my insides didn't perceive the length. Memorable and wonderful all at the same time. It filled me with the satisfied comfort of coming home.

We parted, and he swiped his thumb across my cheek, smiling, before he turned and walked with Ryder toward the fragile beginning stages of finding our way out of this mess.

Chapter 25

My knee bounced as I sat, waiting for movement in the woods. It felt like an eternity had passed since I watched Beck and Ryder walk toward my house. *Where are they? Did they get hurt?*

I couldn't take it anymore. I climbed out of the car, trekking my way to the house. The leaves rustled and crunched under my feet. I cursed inwardly. How did Beck and Ryder make this look so easy?

I attempted to dull the wake of my steps, but all that did was create unbalance and me almost falling on my face. I caught myself and heard a sound. It wasn't from me.

I froze. Shoot! Stupid, so stupid, Alessia.

The soft glow before the sun's official arrival was my only light source as I scanned my surroundings. No movement. It all looked clear. But before I could take another step, a hand grabbed mine.

I screamed.

The hand moved to my mouth while an arm wrapped around me and yanked me close to a warm body.

"Shh."

I looked up into familiar brown eyes and felt a deep relief as my body relaxed into Beck's hold.

I then pushed him away from me. "Don't scare me like that! You could have said something."

"You were supposed to stay in the car." His head tilted, eyeing me.

"You were taking forever, and I got worried."

"It's literally been less than 10 minutes." He shook his head. "C'mon. The house was empty. Ryder is working on securing the entry points." He moved to my side and directed me forward, his hand sliding to the small of my back.

We reached the back porch, climbed the steps, and entered the house. No lights were on, making it feel eerie and empty.

"There's no sign of anyone being here," Beck said as he shut the door.

I walked past him, through the kitchen, and stopped outside my dad's office. Pondering on his whereabouts: Was he safe? Did they bring him back to the States? Was he scared or wondering where I was?

"I think I'll shower if that's okay," I stated absently, staring into the office space.

Ryder trotted down the steps, pulling me from my ruminating.

"All good upstairs. Shall I take the first watch?" He asked, coming into the kitchen.

I headed upstairs, eager to bathe and wear my own clothes again.

"Sure, that might be a good idea. I'll be with Alessia if you need me." Beck responded to Ryder.

Clean and refreshed, I left the bathroom to find Beck sleeping on my bed. I changed into sweatpants and a comfy sweater. Drawing closer to the bed, I watched his chest rise and fall in a slow, rhythmic pattern. His eyes were closed. One hand behind his head and the other on his chest. He looked peaceful. Relaxed and younger. Perfect.

I laid on the bed next to him, grabbed the throw folded at the bottom, and told myself a tiny bit of shut-eye sounded heavenly.

A loud noise startled me awake, and I sat up. The weight of a heavy hand pressed me back into the bed. I looked up, spotting Beck's tousled brown hair.

We were still on my bed, but the peaceful, resting Beck was long gone. He was on high alert; one hand was protectively splayed across me, and the other held his gun towards the door.

"What was that?" I whispered.

He didn't answer. Instead, he moved from the bed and crept over to the door. I jumped up and followed him. He inched the door open. I heard a female squeal, and then...

"Let me go, you big oaf of a man!"

"That's Ava," I said as I sprinted past Beck and raced down the stairs. Beck was hot on my heels, yelling at me to stop.

I stumbled into the living room, Beck hitting my back and grabbing me to steady us both.

Ryder stood not far from the entryway. His hand held a struggling Ava by the wrist. She glared up at him, a lamp broken on the floor behind them.

"Ava," I yelled.

Ava and Ryder both looked at me. Ryder gave me a quizzical look and Ava took advantage of his distracted state to free herself with one final tug and ran into me. Her arms wrapping around me in a hug.

"Oh my gosh! Alessia, where have you been? What is going on?" She pulled back and glanced between the two men in the room. "Did these guys kidnap you?" she whispered.

"No, no, I was not kidnapped....well, not exactly."

"Then what? I knew something was off. Tristan tried to convince me his family was taking care of your disappearance, but he's been acting all tense and weird since it happened. I even tried contacting your dad, but his phone always went to voicemail. I've been worried sick. I started watching the house. I didn't know what else to do. I was just walking around outsi—"

"Explain to me what a tiny little thing like you was going to accomplish sneaking around a house with potential kidnappers," Ryder sniggered, stopping Ava's rambling.

She scoffed, her hands going to her hips. "You don't get to ask me questions."

I grabbed her shoulder, bringing her attention back.

"Ava, listen. Tristan can't be trusted; whatever he told you, he was lying. Beck...well, Beck has been helping me. Ryder, too." I nodded toward Ryder. "Tristan was part of a plan to have me murdered, something involving a money scandal. We're not really sure why—"

"Wait! Murdered? Tristan is trying to kill you? So, the attack? The poison?" Her gaze went unfocused, and her fingers touched her lower lip as she contemplated her questions.

"No, that one was actually Beck. But yes, the attack in the locker room, the library, all of it. Tristan attacked me the night of the benefit and told me he was supposed to eliminate the problem. We think his dad, Lyle, is the one actually behind it. And then Chelsea, who isn't really Chelsea —"

Ava raised a hand, stopping me, and then placed it on her head. "This is a lot. Chelsea? What does she have to do with this?"

"You poisoned her?" Ryder butted in again, looking at Beck.

Beck shifted and rolled his eyes. "It was a safe amount. I had a plan."

"You,"—Ava pointed at Ryder—"stop doing that." She turned back to me. "How do you know you can trust these guys?" she asked, watching them suspiciously.

"They're good. We can trust them." I grabbed both her hands in mine, encouraging her to believe me.

Beck cleared his throat. "Look, there are a lot of details, and some we just don't have time for. How long have you been watching the house? Did you see anyone else around the house?"

"The day after she disappeared. And no, there hasn't been anyone else here. But...."

Ava's phone rang, and she pulled it from her pocket, her screen lighting up with a phone call.

"But what? And why is Tristan calling you?" I asked, trepidation formed in my chest.

"Shoot," she whispered, pressing the phone into her chest

"Ava," I said.

"Alessia, I think...." Her eyes darted around the room. Unshed tears filled them as they finally focused on me pleadingly. "There's something I need to tell you....Tristan. Oh, I promise he said nothing bad was going to happen. At the beginning of school, he asked for my help. To get close to you. I thought he just liked you, but then things got weird, and he just kept saying I needed to keep you away from Beck —"

"What? What do you mean? You were helping him?" I moved back from her. Hurt. Confused. Betrayed.

Her tears finally spilled down her cheeks. "No! No, I didn't know. Please, I didn't know he was going to hurt you. Why would he try to kill you? I didn't help him with anything that happened to you." Her voice cracked.

Ava's phone stopped ringing, and Beck moved into the space between her and me.

"I need you to be very clear and very honest right now," Beck rumbled.

She backed up, head shaking, and bumped into Ryder. "I swear I didn't know," she whispered.

What is happening? Ava is the sweetest person I know. How could she betray me like this?

"But you were helping him. Why is he calling you now," Beck said, his voice rising.

"He's been wanting to know if Alessia has reached out to me....and—"

"And that's why you've been watching for me to come back? Ava, no." I moved around Beck, my own tears now forming. "I thought I could trust you."

"Alessia, you can. All I did was encourage you to give him a chance. When you seemed unsure, I told him so, but he kept pressing. He said I had to help, that Beck was dangerous, and things would go badly if I continued to refuse. I didn't know what to do. It was extremely weird and suspicious, but I didn't think he was the bad guy. I thought he was."—she pointed at Beck—"And he's calling me because....okay, don't hate me. He's calling because I sent him a text saying I saw activity at your house before I came over," she said in a rush.

Beck and Ryder went on full alert, their bodies tensed, poised for a fight. Ryder moved silently toward the door while Beck stepped back, brushing against me.

Ava's phone pinged with a text. She glanced at it, pulling it away from her chest. "He wants to know where I am and what I found at the house. Here, you can read it for yourself." She handed the phone to Beck. He threw her a hard glare, but he took the phone.

Another message came through as I peeked over to read the first one.

Tristan: If Alessia is there, I need to know. And who is with her. And stay out of the house. Trust me, the people she is with are very dangerous. I can help her, though.

"Well, Ava, it looks like you have a choice in front of you. Do you trust whatever story Tristan has fed you, or do you choose to actually start helping your friend," Beck said as he handed the phone back to her.

Ava grabbed the phone to read the message. Her head started shaking back and forth again. "None of this makes any sense. Why would Tristan want Alessia dead? Why would anyone want that?" She looked at each of us in turn.

Her face was genuine, and she looked as puzzled as I felt. I had to believe Ava didn't know what Tristan was up to. She was a victim in his games, just as I was. Beck wouldn't like my next move, but I'd deal with that later. "Message him back to set up a way to meet. I think it's time we find some answers."

Chapter 26

"**W**hoa, what?" Beck said.

I turned to look at him, his face almost comical in a state of horror.

"Do you have a better plan? She has to respond. Or who knows what he'll do. Show up here anyway. Besides, you said we were on the offensive side now," I countered.

"Yeah, but that doesn't mean we use you as bait."

"Who said we were doing that. All I told her to do was message him back." I faced Ava again. "Tell him—"

Her phone received another text.

"He says never mind. Tell Beck to bring her to 347 Windsor Drive tonight before noon, and her father will remain alive. If he fails....," Ava said, reading the message.

Adrenaline spiked. He had my dad? We took too long to figure this out; we needed to do something quick.

"We have to go. He has my dad, Beck," I said, tears pulling in my eyes.

Beck's body tensed, his features darkened, and he looked at me with raw grief. He moved away, his hands reached behind his head and squeezed the hair as he gazed out the window.

Ava moved closer, placing her arm around me in a sideways hug.

"I'm with you. Whatever you want to do, Beck," Ryder vowed.

Beck turned around to face his friend. "We don't know that Oliver is there. We'll go, but not without a plan. Get Ben

221

on the phone. He'll know Dad's ETA. We may be able to hold off until he can help. I also want a layout of this location. And Alessia doesn't leave our side, got it."

Ryder nodded and strolled over to the kitchen island where a laptop sat.

"We can't wait, Beck. We need to go now," I said.

Beck approached me, and Ava moved aside. He placed his palm on my cheek. "Nothing will happen to your dad, and I will die before anything happens to you."

"I can't ask you to make promises you can't keep." I placed my hand on top of his.

"Doesn't matter. Whatever happens next, we fight it together."

"Ben says Marcus and Thalia are arriving in New York in an hour. Plus another four before they make it here. He'll have property blueprints for you in the hour," Ryder yelled from the kitchen.

"Let's get to work," Beck said, leaving my side to join Ryder.

$$\sim$$

I was anxious to get answers and find my dad, which meant I wasn't willing to wait for the Cirillos. Ben sent us images of the property and the home layout. I waited impatiently for Beck and Ryder to design their plan. Beck would stay with me and walk through negotiations with Tristan while Ryder searched for my dad. We tried to convince Ava to keep out of it and wait to hear from us at my house, but she wouldn't relent. Finally, her stubbornness won out, causing Ryder to reluctantly agree she helped him.

We pulled up to the address Tristan gave. A stately home with multiple balconies and windows galore, complete with a gate and a cliche fountain at the center of a circular driveway. It would soon be 11:00, which was too close for comfort.

Beck and I stared at the mansion sprawled out before us. This whole situation seemed counterproductive and messy. It had me on edge. The confident girl who thought she was ready to play hardball was now terrified something might happen to her dad.

A man dressed in a suit greeted us at the stairs, ushering us to the large front doors. Inside, he asked for our coats. When we declined, he nodded and directed us into a sitting room to the right of the main door.

"Ah, Butterfly, you've found your way home." Tristan stood by an elaborate fireplace, his hand resting on the mantle while he gazed at the flames that danced within.

At the sight of Tristan, I wanted to turn and run away. His voice and appearance made my skin crawl. I had no desire to ever be near him again. Beck's hand squeezed mine, the only sign he showed of Tristan's words affecting him.

Tristan turned from the fire, his eyes catching mine before moving to the hand holding Beck's. A smirk appeared on his face. "I knew there was something between you two. I never trusted you, Beckett," he spat the name. "You threw me off at the yacht party. I couldn't figure out your end game, but clearly, I misinterpreted your motives. You actually care for her, don't you," he chortled.

"Where's my dad?" my voice quivered.

"All in due time, love. We have a little business to discuss first."

Beck's hand tightened again, and he moved slightly forward, placing himself between Tristan and me.

"Enough of the games. Who's really behind this, and why are they after Alessia?" Beck demanded.

Tristan chuckled again. "My, Beckett, not even a please. You simply ask a question, and I'm supposed to give it all over? But for this to work, I suppose I do need to bring you up to speed. Our pretty little Alessia, here, doesn't even know the level of interest she holds." His face became devious.

I didn't like that look. This wasn't the direction we needed to go. We needed to be discussing getting my dad.

"I suppose the best place to start is with the case of a missing person. About 22 years ago, Michael Vasili's only daughter, Everlee, disappeared. She left one night and never returned. Even worse, it was the week before her arranged marriage of convenience. But, of course, a man with Vasili's money and power put the best private investigators on the case. Little Everlee evidently was as cunning as her father; they never found her. Vasili never believed her to be dead, though. With his wife's death about a year later, he was left alone without an heir to his inheritance." Tristan moved to the center coffee table and picked up a stack of papers.

"I have here documents confirming Everlee's changed identity and birth of her child. Michael's investigator never found Everlee until she was long dead. He learned of Grace Weber, Everlee's changed name, but this baby was a little bit more hidden. Once Everlee's death was revealed the old man gave up. Grace Weber, your mother, was Vasili's daughter, and she had a child. That child is you, Alessia. Making you the granddaughter of Michael Vasili. The inheritor of *the* Vasili fortune."

Tristan handed the papers to Beck. He returned to the coffee table, grabbed a handful of nuts from a bowl, and popped them in his mouth.

I grabbed the papers from Beck. It was all there. Everything Tristan was saying was true. My mother wasn't who I thought she was. *How is this possible?*

But I didn't have time to sift through those feelings. Tristan had more information I needed.

"So Lyle brought my dad here to kill me and take this inheritance? Why am I here?" I fumed. Angry at the smug arrogance dripping off his every word; his ease of toying with my life.

"Well, look at you. Clever little butterfly. That wasn't how it started," Tristan continued. "But perhaps that's another story for another day.

"No, tell her, Tristan. Tell her how her little tramp of a mother stole my legacy." Andrew appeared out of the shadows on the other side of the room. His thick jet black hair ruffled, and the glare he always gave fixed on me.

Beck pulled me tighter against his side. "We have company," he whispered for the earpiece that connected him to Ryder.

Why was Andrew here, and what did he know about my mom? I continued to listen, quiet, hesitant to receive whatever bomb they planned to drop next.

"Suit yourself," Tristan said. "Christmas four years ago. Poor Andrew is upset about his parents fighting for the final and last time. His parents ended their marriage. But not without revealing a little fun tidbit Andrew latches on to. His dad was bitter and always regretted his missed opportunity to wed Everlee Vasili and gain from her prosperity. Fast forward to the following spring, when a young Tristan and his friend Andrew find solidarity in the desire to make some changes for their future. Though we were young, our hunger and need for power was overwhelming. I learned about Vasili's daughter and whereabouts, digging through my father's office one day. So naturally, when Andrew told me of his plight, we were curious about her and her life. We dug a little deeper. Finding the surprising news about her daughter. We figured it only seemed right for him to meet the girl who stole the future he should have had."

This was getting ridiculous. "You can't be serious. It doesn't even work that way. He may never have been born even if it had gone the other way," I retorted.

Tristan's jaw ticked. "I wasn't finished. We'll have to work on that mouth of yours."

"Her tongue won't be a problem if she is dead," Andrew said.

Tristan grabbed some more nuts. "Back to my story. I had my father arrange a position for Mr. Oliver Weber at Ridgecrest so we could meet the daughter of Everlee Vasili, a.k.a Grace Weber."

"You wanted to kill me at 15?" I shrank closer to Beck.

"Oh, no. We just wanted to play with you." Tristan grinned.

"You did, and you're still playing. I wanted her to pay," Andrew said. "We watched you and waited. You were clueless. You had no idea who you were. The power you had waiting for you. When the old man grew ill this past summer, everything was finally fitting to our needs. We seized our moment. You were the only thing between us and receiving that inheritance. The Vasili estate and fortune would be transferred to the only other partner in Vasili Incorporated. Then Tristan and I would take over. Finally gaining what was rightfully mine."

"Ah, yes. It's good you're here, Andrew," Tristan said. "I was just about to propose a new plan to our sweet Alessia."

I didn't like the sound of that.

Beck's body moved slightly forward as if holding himself back from doing more. "Enough," he growled. "You're both sick and twisted in the head, and we are done with this. What are your terms for releasing Oliver?"

"Not so fast. My father has always spoken so highly of the Verndari Order and appreciates their discreet manner. But I don't appreciate being made a fool, Beckett. I do admire a well-played game, though. And while we all played, I saw a greater opportunity." Tristan sat in a deep navy leather chair. Poised and relaxed. But an edge of something sharp tainted his words.

"No, Tristan. I'm tired of your games. We off her and be done with it," Andrew said.

Tristan laughed. "Oh, Andrew. You should have realized I was the one holding all the cards. Unless I go into a partnership with you. There is nothing for you. And why share all that wealth." He snapped his fingers, and a man dressed all in black walked in, shooting Andrew in the head.

Blood splattered.

A scream burst from my lips, and Beck's hold on me intensified as he moved us backward.

Andrew's body collapsed to the floor. A pool of blood forming on the floor next to it.

Tristan's gaze focused on us. "Alessia will legally bind herself to me through marriage, and her father lives. Refuse, and I will kill you both right now." He sat back, spreading his arms behind him, his leg lifted to rest on the other.

Three more men came into the room surrounding us.

"I told you, Beckett, I'm not a very nice enemy to have. You should have done your job. Now, you'll have to watch her be mine," Tristan sneered.

A sick feeling plummeted in my stomach.

"We have more company. What's your status?" Beck sent another more urgent whisper through his earpiece. He leaned back toward me. "Ava took off. She said something about knowing what to do. Ryder didn't go after her. He's found nothing and is on his way here." Beck's face held concern.

Then his arm encircled my waist as he moved us closer to a window. Was he going to try to escape through the window?

I tried to tell myself that Beck and Ryder were trained for this and knew what to do in unexpected situations. But at the moment, I didn't see how even they could get us out of this.

"Take them out back. Make it quick and quiet. We'll hide her body before letting it be discovered in a ditch somewhere," Tristan said, getting up from his chair and leaving the room.

Bile once again filled my stomach. What would cause people to value the life of another human so callously?

"And the boy?" one of the armed men asked.

"Boys. There's another one lurking about. Find him. And it's a causality of their job. It won't be a problem," Tristan hollered over his shoulder.

Two of the men left the room, and the other two moved forward. Beck continued to the window. I could feel his heart beating fast against me.

We were up against the wall. Literally and figuratively. This wasn't going to end well. There had to be a better way.

"Wait," I yelled. But Beck had other plans. His elbow went into the window behind us.

The loud shattering noise of glass breaking muffled my shout. Beck adjusted to push me out the window, but not before the sound of a gun pierced the air, and his hold on me loosened.

Chapter 27

"**B**eck," I screamed, turning to face him.
His right hand reached to grab my waist again, pushing me toward the broken window. A sharp hiss left his mouth.

I glanced at his left arm, where blood collected and dripped.

"It's fine. It's just a graze," he whispered.

The large man in black holding a gun moved forward. His rough hands grabbed me, trying to pull me from Beck's loose grip. I was so focused on Beck I forgot the other people in the room.

Beck moved then, faster than I would have imagined, and slammed his fist into the guy who grabbed me, knocking him to the side, disorienting him. The other guy came from behind and wrapped a burly arm around Beck's neck. And I fell out of his reach.

Beck threw his elbow into the man's face, causing him to topple back, but he seized Beck's injured arm as he fell. Beck cried out in pain and stumbled to stay upright as the guy held firm. Agony etched his face. It was breaking my heart. I needed to do something.

The first guy came back, hitting Beck in the stomach. Not once, but three times. *No.* I could see him growing tired, and he was in pain.

With a burst of energy, Beck's knee rammed into the guy in front of him. Beck twisted his arm, gaining the upper hand. The man's eyes widened right before Beck painfully

Beck's hand grazed my boot as he reached for the gun we hid there. He moved in front of me and pressed the gun into the temple of the man next to me. At the same time, the man positioned his gun toward my stomach.

Heavy pants exchanged around our precarious circle. I could tell Beck's arm was giving him trouble. We weren't going to last much longer.

A big part of me wanted a miraculous escape to somehow happen. To not have to deal with any of the hard and difficult situations we were suddenly facing. And yet another part of me knew that wasn't likely.

The reality of death being imminent seeped into my very bones.

But as I glanced at Beck, I didn't want this to be the end. He deserved so much more. He had done so much for me. Cared deeply. He showed me living was worth fighting for. Helped me realize that if I continued to hide from painful realities, it would only put off the inevitable.

Burying things, running from emotions, and acting as if they weren't affecting my daily life kept me from living. Hiding and keeping secrets would always keep me lost. Lost from love. Lost from processing the pain. Lost from the truth. My mother hid, but her secrets finally caught up to her.

Through me.

Beck's words from self-defense training returned to me: *Your goal isn't to fight the attacker but to fight the attacker's objective.*

My eyes closed. Deep breath in. Slow breath out. *One, two, three...*

Opening my eyes, I saw the back of Tristan's figure continue to walk away.

"Tristan," I yelled.

He glanced over his shoulder. A sick smile appeared.

"Your plan won't work. You can't manipulate this situation in your favor. Killing me eliminates one problem, but too many know now. What's your plan to silence all those mouths?" I challenged. "One leak that you murdered the Vasili heir, and you lose it all."

In my peripheral, Beck's eyes flickered in my direction, his fingers tightening on his weapon, and the man with his gun on me winced, his own hold wavering.

"I'm nothing if not determined," Tristan said, turning around and strolling toward us.

But his demeanor shifted. His countenance uncertain.

He didn't even question my bluff. Seeds of doubt hit their target; he was faltering in his confidence.

"Do you know how people become great? How they build an empire?" he said.

I remained silent, holding his stare.

"They take it. They claim it." He drew closer. Each step heavier than the last. "Vasili's empire is mine. Your mother didn't want anything to do with it. And I bet you're exactly the same. Fine, you detach yourself from the Vasili name, granting me all rights and inheritance."

Tristan loved his games, and he was playing a similar game to mine, counting on my weaknesses: My fears of losing everything if I didn't surrender to his demands.

Beck's body trembled next to me, and his injured arm gave out, losing his grip on the man behind him. That small movement caused a rapid chain reaction.

The man behind Beck fell, cradling his arm. Beck's gun slipped, allowing the bulky man next to him to lunge forward and ram the butt of his gun against Beck's head.

Beck swayed back and was knocked to the ground. But the guy didn't stop there. He pounced on Beck and began slamming his fists into Beck's face.

Recklessness and impulsivity reigned in my next thought. Banking on the shock value to work in my favor. I bent down and grabbed a sharp piece of glass, the edges cutting into my palm. My arm drew back and forced the sharp edge into the shoulder of the man attacking Beck. He roared in anger, his hand swatting at his back as if the shard of glass was a fly.

A bit astonished, my feet stumbled back, bumping into a firm body. Tristan's hand grabbed my wrist and twisted it to the near point of breaking. I screamed in pain.

"Lissa," Beck yelled, rolling over to spit blood from his mouth as he attempted to pull himself off the floor.

"I'm disappointed you're so unwilling to make this work. We could have had so much fun together," Tristan hissed in my ear. My wrist throbbed, the pain making it hard to see.

Shots fired, and a soft thud sounded near me. Tristan's hand fell away as his body stumbled backward. Looking back, I saw blood spilling onto his shirt near his shoulder.

I staggered away. Scared. Shocked. Numb.

My footsteps found Beck. He was pale, sweat built along his brow while he rested on one knee, a gun in his left hand.

Ryder raced into the room, carrying a silenced pistol, and two more dull thuds took down the men around Beck.

"Beck." I reached for him, grabbing his face. "Beck," I said. Fear struck me and leaked into my voice. "Beck, look at me. Tell me you're okay." A heavy sigh was his only response as his eyes fell shut. I inspected his arm, which was still bleeding.

Ryder toppled another body, knocking out another security guard. He rushed to our side, took one look at Beck, and whipped off his belt. Moving me to the side, he tightened the makeshift tourniquet around Beck's arm. My hand went to Ryder's shoulder. "He's okay, right," I asked.

Ryder's eyes roved over Beck's face and body. "He will be." He lifted Beck's arm over his shoulder and began walking out of the room. I quickly followed him.

"Wait," Tristan gurgled. "You're just—going to leave me?"

Ryder didn't stop. He kept walking in the direction we came in.

Tristan paled and fumbled to the couch.

"Shouldn't we do something? He's going to die," I said, referring to Tristan.

"It was either you or him. And Beck is Verndari. He protects. Sometimes that requires the life of another."

We made it to the car. Ryder helped Beck into the backseat, and I crawled next to him. His eyes were still shut, and his head lolled to the side.

Pressing my palm to his cheek, I moved his face to look at me, a face that held some of my most treasured memories. A face I never wanted to see another day without. "Beck, listen to me. You have to stay with me, okay? Because I don't know what's going to happen in the future or even what's about to happen next. All I know is I love you, and I want you by my side. I need you by my side."

Beck's hand moved then, squeezing my leg. I smiled, and my chest filled with relief. *He's still with me.*

"What now," I asked Ryder.

"His wound needs to be patched. I know a place, but it's a bit away. Keep talking to him. See that he stays with us."

"And my dad?"

Ryder caught my eye in the mirror and shook his head. We didn't find him. An ache throbbed in my chest as my worry for where he was and his safety grew. I wouldn't let it deter our current trajectory, though. We would keep searching for him once Beck was taken care of, as well as figure out what to do with the information overload I just received. *My mom had a secret identity?*

I turned my gaze from him to out the window. The evening didn't go as we thought. Not at all how we wanted it, but it did bring an end.

Tristan wanted to be the master of the game, but like most people with power, he saw himself as invincible. As if he was beyond paying for his wrong actions. But truth will always reveal hidden secrets; we can only run for so long before lies and wicked deeds catch up to us. And Tristan pushed till he found himself on the wrong end of the equation.

Chapter 28

We pulled into the gravel driveway of a small house with green siding and a metal blue roof, nestled on a large plot of land and a forest of trees. It looked nice enough, but Beck seriously needed help, and I didn't like the looks of our options here.

"Ryder, if you're taking him to some sketchy place to get fixed up, I'm not okay with that," I argued, sitting up and letting go of Beck's hand.

He turned around. "Listen, girl scout, Beck and his family mean more to me than you'll ever understand. I'm taking care of him," he said gruffly.

I nodded. "Okay."

"Okay."

Ryder opened the door and came to the back to help Beck just as an older muscular man with several tattoos covering his arms walked out of the house.

"Ryder?" the man asked.

"Hey, Keith. I need some work done on a bullet wound. Beck's been hit and bleeding for a while now."

"Who's Keith," I said as the man moved closer.

"An old friend."

I eyed him as he helped Ryder with Beck while I quietly followed them, hoping I wasn't about to lose one of the most important people in my life.

They brought him into one of the bedrooms and made me wait by the door facing the bed. After close to an hour, they finally finished their work on his arm and allowed me to move next to him.

He was asleep, and his breathing was steady. All the blood was cleaned up, but the swelling on his face had become more prominent. Even still, his striking features amazed me. He was beautiful in so many ways.

Brushing his hair back, he leaned into my hand, and I rested my head next to his. We were together. Together, in a moment of peace after the devastatingly horrific ordeal we just endured.

I woke to voices speaking in loud whispers outside the room. Soft, squishy material engulfed my body, along with strong arms. I was no longer on the chair next to the bed but on the bed, wrapped close to Beck.

My slight movement must have awoken him because when I tilted my head slightly and met those enchanting brown eyes, they were open and full of so much more life than the last time I looked into them.

"Hi," he said, smiling

"Hi."

Inner tingles assaulted me. "How are you feeling?"

"Much better now," he mumbled as he pulled me closer and nuzzled my neck.

A giggle escaped me, and I pushed him back slightly. "Really? You were shot, Beck. And losing consciousness." I gave him a dubious look.

He smiled again and shrugged. "Minor details. It wasn't the first time."

I rolled my eyes. "It wasn't the first time," I repeated, mocking him. "You're ridiculous," I said and started to move off the bed.

"You're ridiculous if you think I'm going to let you off this bed now that I have you here." He laughed and grabbed my waist, pulling me back against him. Both smiling, his hand found my wrist, his thumb caressed over it. "And your wrist?"

Our eyes met, and I pressed a hand to his cheek.

"You saved me," I whispered.

A throat cleared from the doorway. Our heads turned in unison.

"Ava called. Gave us an address to meet her at," Ryder said.

"Ava?" I asked, crawling out of Beck's hold and off the bed.

"Yeah, when she took off back at that house, she said she'd call when she had what we needed," he said, shrugging.

"Well, what did she say? What does she mean by what we need?"

"All she said was to meet her at this address. Also, Marcus and Thalia just arrived. They'll be wanting to see you." He handed me a piece of paper with writing scrawled on it, nodded at Beck, and walked away.

I turned around, facing Beck, who was now sitting up on the bed. "What do you think it means?" I asked.

I trusted Ava. I didn't think she meant me any harm, but her taking off and now giving random addresses felt off. *Did she know where Dad was?*

"Beckett. Alessia." Thalia's lithe form entered the room and pulled me in for a hug before she moved past me to examine Beck.

"Mom, it's fine," Beck said while his mother pressed gently at his arm.

She gave him a stern look. "I'd feel better about that if I would have been the one to work on it."

He rolled his eyes. "Keith is good. You know that." His gaze drifted to me. "If you trust her. I trust her."

"Trust who," Thalia questioned, looking between us.

"Then we go and see what she knows," I said.

When we finished thanking and saying goodbye to Keith, it was late morning, and it seemed like the night before was ages ago. Yet, all of it still swirled in my thoughts like smoke —floating up clear and tangible until vanishing, and I'm left unable to fully grasp the situation.

The truth bomb Tristan dropped, fighting for our lives, Beck getting hurt, all leading to no idea where my dad was or what to do with the new knowledge of who I was. *One step forward with two steps back.*

Thalia and Marcus weren't about to let us jump into another unknown position alone. They joined us, Thalia driving us to a large mansion. One I instantly recognized because it was the Dufort mansion where the benefit was held, but none of the glamour from that evening dressed the house. Instead, a cop car blocked the short driveway, and several unmarked cars were parked near the house's main entrance.

"This is the address she gave?" I asked Ryder.

"It appears to be," he answered, leaning forward to assess the area around the house.

Beck's body tensed beside me, but he moved forward as if prepping for the worst. "Stop here," he said.

Thalia put the car in park but left the engine running. From the front seat, Marcus turned to face Beck and Ryder, sitting on either side of me. "I don't know what is happening here, but Alessia requires our care. Whatever is going on, she is the priority."

"Yeah. Glad you've caught on to that," Beck said

"If someone would have included us in more detail earlier on, that would have looked different, Beckett," Thalia remarked with a slight smile. The corners of Beck's lips lifted as he responded with a head shake.

"Ready?" He nodded to Ryder.

"Not without me, you don't," I insisted.

"Your fight. I just fight it with you," Beck said. He grabbed my hand to pull me out of his side of the car with him, but he dropped it suddenly, and I bumped into his back from the abrupt stop in movement. A man in uniform from the cop car was approaching us.

"This is a private investigation. I'm going to have to ask you to turn around and leave," the officer said, hesitant about our presence.

"Sorry, officer. We were looking for someone," I said around Beck's shoulder.

"Well, this just got interesting," Ryder spoke calmly, coming up behind me. *Not the word choice I was thinking.*

A short blonde bounced out from one of the SUVs parked near the house and raced over.

"That's Ava," I said, astonished and confused. She pushed past Beck and quickly enfolded me into her arms. "Oh, you're okay," she whispered in my ear.

"Ava, what—"

She pulled back from our hug. "Right. When Ryder and I were looking for your dad, he rudely snapped at me, telling me to be quiet because he was trying to hear what Tristan was saying to you guys through the earpiece. He caught that Tristan was talking about Vasili and his missing daughter and something about your mom. It didn't take me long to piece it together. It was a huge deal when Michael Vasili's daughter disappeared all those years ago. So much so it's been a hot topic at my parent's annual summer gathering for years. You know, the one they invite all the major playing lawyers in the New York and upper East Coast area to. Anyway, I've met Vasili's lawyer before. I knew if I got him involved, he would be able to help. And here we are, ready to help." She clapped her hands together, quite proud of herself. "Sorry it took so long. These guys didn't want to listen to me until I had the actual lawyer call." Rolling her eyes, she waved her hand at the house, where an older, well-groomed man in a beige blazer and matching pants now stood at the top of the stairs leading to the front door.

"That's Nathaniel Bence. He's the top business and estate lawyer in New York and has worked for the Vasili family for over 30 years. He's eager to meet you."

"He is? What's going on? Why are we here, and how did you accomplish all of this?"

She waved her hand at me like it was no big deal. "Please, if my parents have taught me anything, people love a good scandal, especially when big money is involved: like moths to a flame. Nathaniel says Vasili and Dufort have been at odds for some time now. Vasili was suspicious of accounting documents coming out of Dufort's investments. There were threats of cutting Dufort out of the company altogether. With attempts on your life as a Vasili heir, Nathaniel had enough to start an official investigation."

"Did they find Tristan? And Andrew?" I asked.

Her lips turned down. "The police have reported 4 dead bodies at the Fenton house," she said. Her head shaking. "I don't know whose, but if they were there..."

They would be dead.

Nathaniel started in our direction, and the police officer retreated back to his post. Marcus and Thalia got out, joining our group.

Beck's posture hardened. Dominating. Threatening. Ready to protect what was his.

"Can she trust him?" he asked, eyeing Nathaniel's approach.

"Does she need to when she has you? All of you?" Ava said, admiring the group. "Yeah, he's good. He'll honor the family name. Which means she's his new boss."

My eyes widened at the realization of Ava's statement. Everything was about to change.

"Miss Weber," Nathaniel said. His hand extended in greeting. I shook it in response. "Nathaniel Bence, of Bence and Latham. I believe I have good news for you. We've located your father. He's here."

"What?" I was not expecting that. An intense weight I didn't even realize I was carrying lifted. "You found him? How? Is he okay? Can I talk to him?"

"We're still investigating, but it appears Tristan's mother may be an accomplice to his plans. I'll have someone inform your father you're here," he replied, motioning for the patrol car officer to come over. "Please find Mr. Weber and tell him he is needed out front. His daughter is here."

The officer left in the direction of the house.

"Investigations?" I asked.

"I'm a very skilled lawyer, Miss Weber, who worked for an exceptionally powerful man. I've been waiting far too long to unearth Lyle Dufort's secrets. You, my dear, appear to be my catalyst. I realize you have been through quite the ordeal in recent hours. While I would love to answer all your questions, there are questions I need answered. I believe you are who our mutual friend here says you are, but before I can officially stand in your corner, we need to confirm who you are." He handed me a card. "This is how you can reach me. On the back is the address of the Vasili Manor. I need you to meet me there at 2:00 pm today. I'll have personnel ready for a DNA swab and a reading of the will."

This was really happening.

A moment later, I saw Dad being assisted down the house's main entrance stairs. Seeing him, I started crying and rushed over to him. I could sense Beck following behind.

"Dad. Oh, Dad, you're okay." I squeezed around his neck, and his arm pulled me in.

"I'm okay. I'm just glad you're okay," he said.

I pulled back and nodded. Tears still fell. A mix of relief and sadness.

"What have they told you?" I asked.

"I'm not sure very much. Police officers showed up this morning, and a man dressed in a fine suit told me my daughter's life was threatened because she's the granddaughter of Michael Vasili. I'm going to need filling in, I think."

"You have no idea, Dad. There's so much. And Beck. You remember the Cirillos, right?" I grabbed Beck's hand and pulled him close.

Dad's head dipped in greeting. "The Cirillos? Why are the Cirillos here?" He paused. "Ah, and the past finds our future. This is about your mother."

"Wait. You knew who she was? And the Cirillos?" My mouth fell open.

"She held the details close, but I knew she had a life before me that she was running from. And all I know of the Cirillos is they were always very protective of you. Thalia reached out to me a couple times after we moved to ask

242

about you. I couldn't figure out why, but if they're here now, I'm guessing there was a deeper reason for that protectiveness. " He grabbed my free hand. "She was the woman you remember, though, Lessy. This is a big change, but it doesn't change who she was."

"It is a lot. It's going to take some time." I glanced up at Beck, and he smiled back. "But I'm not feeling so afraid of that."

Epilogue

8 months later

"**A**lessia, you 'bout ready?" Ava walked up behind the vanity I sat at. I stared into the mirror one last time and turned to face her.

"We're going to be late, heiress. I mean, I know your life is a whole other level these days, but you were the one who wanted to attend graduation," she teased.

I was the Vasili heir, and that changed everything.

My final year at Ridgecrest turned into a crazy ride of almost dying, finding my best friend and myself, to becoming the most desired person in the world. Everyone wanted in my pockets. Makes sense when one inherits billions.

Life became different. I still attended the Academy but also missed a lot to travel for banquets or special meetings. I suddenly was required for the final say in so many decisions. I wasn't left to figure it out all on my own, though. Forget calculus. I had a financial team educating me to oversee all my new assets. But aside from all the new, I still wanted a piece of normal.

"I'm ready." I stood and released a freeing exhale. "We're graduating, Ava." I grinned, squealing, and grabbed her hands. She, of course, sprang into action, squealing with me.

"Whoa, you two need to chill before Beck hears and thinks someone is attacking his poor, sweet Alessia," Ben said, making a mocking, sad face.

Things changed for the Cirillo family, too. They took over managing the Vasili security team. The whole family moved into the four-level 16,000 square foot Georgian mansion I earned possession of at the reading of the will. While Dad and I chose the more subtle option of the two—the two-story guest house.

Tilting my head at him as he slid over the arm of the loveseat at the end of my bed, I said, "I'm telling him you said that."

"Good. I could use a good fight from him. Conrad's too easy."

"Okay, help me get this on without wrecking everything." I handed Ava my cap.

"Of course," she said.

"And there she stands, this radiant beauty for all to admire and congratulate." Beck walked through the door. His eyes scanning and appreciative. "And somehow, she's all mine."

Ava finished pinning the cap, a giant smile spread across my lips, and a mass amount of butterflies infiltrated my belly.

Having the Cirillos back in my life helped me realize the crucial benefit of having others willing to stick through the fire with you. Their support and care emboldened me. They wanted to journey with me. See me overcome and survive. It made me feel so much stronger than if I was alone.

Beck moved closer, circling his arms at my waist. My arms found their way around his neck.

"What makes you so sure I'm yours?" I asked.

"I've got a good sense about these things." He winked.

"And are you all mine, Beckett Cirillo?"

He bit his bottom lip, debating. "Not that easy. Because something in those eyes melts me every time, and I crave it. I need it." He pulls me in tighter. "My life is better with you in it. I plan to protect and hold on to that as long as I can. Savor every moment. Seize every kiss." He kissed me lightly. Teasingly. Deliciously.

My eyes fluttered shut.

"But more than that, you deserve someone who won't leave your side. Who counts you as more important than themselves. I will fail at that, Lissa. But I will never stop striving for it," he continues in a whisper across my lips. And then closed the distance, meeting me more than halfway. His hands dug into my hair, and I tugged him back with just as much fervor, deepening the kiss.

It never failed. Kissing Beck was like swiping a match and catching fire to everything inside me. Igniting a passion in me to be stronger. To push through the messy and find the better. To remain hopeful even in the dark.

It was stupid to think all the pieces of me didn't already belong to him. Fighting against it was a battle I'm glad I lost.

He pulled back, still gripping my waist.

"Gross, get a room, you two." Ben threw a pillow at us.

Beck easily deflected it. "We're in a room. You need to leave the room," he said.

"No more pillows. You'll mess up her hair," Ava chided.

Beck picked up the pillow and whipped it back at his brother. Ben jumped, dodging it, and raced for the door. Beck ran after him, a huge smile on his face and a tint of hunger in his eyes.

"I don't know how you're going to live this close to so many obnoxious boys. And be sure to always tell me when that Ryder guy is visiting so I know not to come around those days," Ava grumbled.

"Awe, come on, Ryder is great."

"Great at being a turd."

I laughed and grabbed my clutch from the vanity.

Beck's head popped in from the hallway. "You coming?" he asked. His face bright. Reminding me of days from our childhood. Wherever Beck was, that's where I wanted to be. He was and would always be mine. And for the first time in a long time, I no longer felt alone.

Thank you!

This book wouldn't be possible without you. Thank you so much for taking a ride with me on Alessia and Beck's story. I love their sweet relationship so much. I hope you fell in love with them, too. Don't forget to leave a review so others can find my book!! I would greatly appreciate your kindness!

About the Author

Wenna loves a good love story and wants to share that love with others. And so she did. Wenna is a fiction writer and goes wherever the pen leads her. Right now, she is building stories with a blend of mystery and romance and looks forward to seeing where that road takes her. When she isn't writing, she homeschools her two children, dances in her kitchen, or cozy on the couch reading a book.

For updates on all Wenna's books follow her @author.wennaolsson on Instagram

Acknowledgments

So many to thank on this journey of publishing an actual fiction novel.

God is the one who gifted me with not only the ability to write but revealed to me a love for words. The hope and transformation within them are why I love them so. He will always be my source of understanding.

My husband. You showed support even without ever reading a word. I don't know how you were so confident in my skills, but you always seem to know how to convince me I can do something without me even realizing you are doing it.

My son, Eli, you will forever be my biggest encourager. Your excitement for my writing and building a story is unmatched and kept me going when I felt at my worst. You are my bubby. Always stay golden.

My daughter, Olivia, your love is felt in everything you do and say. Your support will always be needed in my life.

Krystale, I've told you before, and I'll say it over and over. This book would not have made it this far without you. Your constant encouragement. Your eagerness for the next chapter. How you understood the story so well, even in the messy drafting attempts. You were with the story from the beginning and will always be its biggest fan.

Kailia, you are amazing! And made Alessia and Beck really come alive and helped me find their story, not just the plot. Thank you, thank you for all your help in the very beginning stages of this amazing journey. You have a gift for storytelling, and I can't wait to see where it takes you.

Liz and Ania—you know!

Salah, your love for the story helped me in some very needed times. When the words weren't there for me, your excitement kept me going.

Amanda, your encouragement and friendship are such a gift in my life. I love that you loved the story. And that I had you cheering me on. It was so needed!

Special shoutout to all my camp girls and Motel 4 and our beautiful story times. You guys loved the story, even with my terrible reading skills.

My beta readers, your eyes found all the things mine couldn't. You helped sharpen my writing, create more immersion, and build an amazing story. I can't thank you enough.

Made in the USA
Middletown, DE
31 October 2023